APPLE SIGN

STAY

Short Stories for Strong Girls

TRUE

COMPILED AND EDITED BY MARILYN SINGER

SCHOLASTIC INC.
New York Toronto London Auckland Sydney
Mexico City New Delhi Hong Kong

To strong girls everywhere

✶   ✶   ✶   ✶   ✶

ISBN 0-590-36033-7

All rights reserved. Published by Scholastic Inc. SCHOLASTIC, APPLE, and associated logos are trademarks and/or registered trademarks of Scholastic Inc.

12 11 10 9 8 7 6 5 4 3 2 1   9/9 0 1 2 3 4/0

Printed in the U.S.A.   40

First Scholastic paperback printing, March 1999

Book design by Elizabeth B. Parisi

CONTENTS

Taking Toll

Albert C. Cooksley is Mom's latest boyfriend. He's been on the scene for over a year now. He likes to think of himself as my dad. He's always saying, "Whatever you need, Princess, you come to me. I'll do my darnedest to get it for you." His eyes, shy and toad-colored, meet mine, blink, and look away. He jingles the loose change in his pocket.

What he has no idea of is that he can never be my father. He's a nice enough person. In fact he's too nice. It's hard to hate someone who's so nice. But I do my best.

"How can you hook up with someone like Albert?" I ask Mom when it sinks in from a conversation I've eavesdropped on that he's going to be a permanent fixture, like the wall stain over the couch.

Mom, in her slip, is on her unmade bed getting

ready to go to work. She has her panty hose in her hand, inspecting it for a run. "And what's wrong with Albert? He's a perfectly nice man." She pushes the gooseneck lamp away so she can see me better. "Why aren't you ready for school, Miranda? They don't like all those tardies, you know. That one . . . Sister whatever —"

"Immaculate," I fill in. That isn't really her name — it's what we call her. Her real name is Mary Claire.

"She calls me at *work* — a personal call — you know how Mr. Lawston *hates* personal phone calls — to tell me that you're always late and that sometimes you don't even show up at all." Mom holds me in the solemn beam of her hazel eyes and I feel trapped — as if one of those shopping center spotlights is holding me in place. "If you don't get educated, you'll end up like me. You don't want that, do you?" There is a quick shine of tears, gone almost before I even register them.

"You didn't end up so bad." I swallow and reach out to touch her bare shoulder, but she's already bent over and is struggling into her panty hose. My hand flies stupidly through air.

Her big toe, the nail painted bright plum, rams through the end of the stocking. "Oh, shoot," she says. "Get me . . ."

I reach into the top drawer of her dresser and

hand her another sealed package before she can finish her sentence.

"Thank you. Now go on. Get dressed."

I turn and am halfway to the door when she speaks again.

"Albert treats me like I'm the only woman in the world," she says. Her voice is soft.

"He's a toll taker, Mom."

"And I'm a restaurant hostess," she says. "Big deal. Since when have you gotten so snooty?"

"You're a singer, waiting for a break, not a hostess," I say fiercely, reminding her of the dream she's told me ever since I was big enough to hear a bedtime story. "Albert's —"

"Albert's not dumb," she says, guessing — correctly — at what I'm thinking, but she sounds unsure. I know I have planted the beginning of the end of Albert C. Cooksley. It won't be long before Albert is history like Len, Mitchell, and Jase. If it hadn't been for me, Mom wouldn't have realized that Len just pretended to be job hunting while he was living with us. He went to cheap afternoon movies instead. Mitchell had another woman. It took me a long time to find something to unseat Jase. And even then I had to stretch. Sometimes I think getting rid of Jase was a mistake. Mom took it hard. She still hasn't gotten her fire back after dumping him.

Lureen and Betty are already at the bus stop when

I get there. Riding the bus to school has turned into my biggest nightmare since Mom began dating Albert because we have to go over the bridge. So far as I know from the questions I've asked he's never manned the truck and bus entrance to the bridge. But there's always a first time. I just know he'd wave like he knew me.

Once the three of us are jammed in a seat, Betty starts talking about where we'll go on our lunch break. Before Albert I never had money to eat out with Betty and Lureen. Albert's taken to leaving coins stacked up in two little neat piles next to my place at the table every morning.

The bus swings wide, and suddenly we're at the top of the hill approaching the toll plaza. I can't see the people taking toll yet; the cars themselves are smaller than matchbox toys. Albert should be in the third booth from the right — that's what he's told me. He gets mildly annoyed when I call him a toll taker. He says he's a bridge officer.

I imagine him standing in a booth that is so small he can't bend to tie his shoe. The booths have been redone recently — made smaller to conserve space. Although he doesn't like this, Albert takes it in stride like he takes everything. Two of his old-time buddies have quit over it, one because he was too fat.

"If you were too fat to fit, what would you do?" I asked him.

"Diet," he answered. He'd reached over and helped himself to more mashed potatoes. "'Course I've never had a problem like that. As you can see, food doesn't land on this frame for long."

He loves to tell of the emergencies he's handled — the sights he's seen. Naked people. Crazy people. One woman tried to give him her baby for the toll. Dangerous people. "The abuse I have to take," Albert says, letting out a sigh. "It isn't like it used to be when people brought you the first apricots of the season."

Mom clucks and looks at him like he's some kind of hero. And he gets that shy, proud, tucked-in smile as if every day in the tollbooth is like going to the front line in a war.

When the bus rolls up to the booth, I let go of the pen I keep for this emergency. It plunks onto the floor and slides under the seat.

"How come you can't keep a hold of that thing?" Lureen asks. "You drop it every day."

Not answering, I fumble around her shoes for it. I keep my head low until I can tell we're on the bridge. Then I straighten up and breathe.

"You're getting weirder and weirder, Miranda," Lureen observes. "It's getting hard to be your friend you're getting so weird."

"So be somebody else's. You've got *so* many to choose from."

"Come on, guys, don't fight," Betty begs. Betty is the person who links us together. Lureen and I wouldn't be friends in a million years if it wasn't for Betty.

"You two going to the Freshman Sports Fair Saturday?" Betty asks. It's for fathers and daughters. She's asked Lureen and me that every day for the last week. Much as I like Betty, she can be insensitive. I feel Lureen stiffen beside me. Neither Lureen nor I have fathers. I mean, I, at least, had one once; I don't know if Lureen *ever* had one. I suspect by how prickly she gets at the mention of fathers that she didn't. Both of us hate the idea of this annual event.

"No," Lureen says right off.

I hunch my shoulders. "Actually, I think the thing is kind of stupid. I mean, it was all right when I was seven or nine —"

"But now that you're almost fourteen, you're too old?" Lureen interrupts.

"Something like that," I lie. Sports are the one thing I'm really good at. I hold the school's record for the long jump and I'm second in the hundred-meter hurdles. My mother's never seen me compete. Sports just aren't her thing. My athletic ability must have come from my dad.

A glance at Lureen tells me she isn't fooled. Betty is. She's already rattling on. I can only catch every few words. The bus has hit the worn patches on an up-

MARION DE BOOY WENTZIEN

grade in the highway. The gears grind. It shakes and roars. I try to imagine asking Albert to go with me. *No way!* I think.

Mom keeps a picture of my father, Russell Harvey, inside her dresser under her underwear. He was in the Navy and stationed here. Mom met him at a dance and dropped out of high school to marry him five days later. According to her, they were married exactly sixteen months. He was sent somewhere, she seems unclear where, and she's never heard from him since. She never bothered to get divorced. I don't think she bothered to track him down, either. Mom tends to procrastinate about things.

Sometimes when I am feeling sorry for myself, which isn't as much as it used to be, I pull out his picture and look at it. He only looks about four years older than I am now. In the picture he has a faraway look in his eyes and a stubborn chin. I expect he found marriage, a baby, and debts more than any eighteen-year-old has a right to be buried under. Mom, when she talks about him, which is only after she's had three glasses of red wine, says he had big plans. For a long time I thought she meant like being an Olympic track star or one of the Blue Angels.

Then I made the mistake of asking her. "Yeah, Russell had big plans all right," she agreed darkly. "Like robbing a bank. Listen, you might as well get any fantasy you have about *him* straight out of your head. He was a big talker — that's what he was. And he liked big trouble. He's either in jail or dead. One or the other doesn't matter to me. Just don't go telling me he was some kind of wonderful because that he wasn't. I was just too young and *ignorant* to know it at the time. So here I am and here you are. And we've made the best of it. Albert's a nice guy. So quit comparing him to Russell. I want you to like him."

I just can't. He's too real — like you can see his bones and each breath he takes. Then there's the way he shines his shoes so that you can almost see your face in them.

"How's life treating you, Princess?" Albert asks late that afternoon when he comes in after work. He tosses his uniform jacket over the back of the couch where I am sitting watching TV. His shoes look just as shiny as they did this morning. He's carrying a paper bag. I can tell by the smell it's crab — crab and French bread, which is getting to be Wednesday night dinner.

Mom is thrilled by the fact that Albert brings in dinner half the nights of the week and she doesn't have to cook. Most of the guys she's hung around with haven't been enthusiastic about women's lib. They think a woman should work and cook. They think a guy should lie around and be waited on.

I want him to stay in the kitchen, but, of course,

he comes in and sits down on the couch next to me. It's too much effort to get up, snap off the TV, and go into my room; otherwise I would, if for no other reason than to *show* Albert C. once and for all we are not buddies or friends or whatever else he's hoping we'll be.

He settles into watching the game show I'm watching. Len used to make *me* change to sports whenever he plunked his fat fanny down. My sideways glances take in the fact that there are damp half-moons under Albert's arms — he's got his hands folded behind his head. According to him, the booth is either too hot or too cold — nothing in between. Evidently today it was hot.

"A guy bit me today," he says in a low voice, not looking at me, just watching the toothpaste commercial as if it were the most important thing in the world.

"Bit you?" I say, amazed in spite of myself.

"Yeah. I reach for his toll and all of a sudden he grabs my hand, bares my wrist, and takes a bite."

Albert rolls back his tan sleeve and sure enough there's the shape of a human mouth on either side of his brown wrist. A couple of the teeth marks are deep and filled in with purple. Only the two front teeth seemed to have broken the skin and those narrow pockets have dried blood in them.

"I sure hope he don't have AIDS. I don't think

I'll tell your mother. She'll get all upset. I probably shouldn't have told you. Don't you tell her, Princess. Okay?"

"Did you *tell* someone?" I ask, not answering his question. I can't believe he let someone bite him and then just stood there taking tolls, saying, "Have a good day." I'm not sure that's what he says, but it sounds like the kind of thing he would. He's very polite.

"Like who?" He seems confused by my question. His forehead has crumpled up like a plowed field. "He was out of there before I could *do* anything. He was driving a Volvo station wagon." Albert is shaking his head now, his eyes wide with disbelief. "I'd never think the driver of a Volvo would bite. I wasn't even *prepared* for anything bad. A VW bus, a black Caddy, a low rider, I brace myself, but a Volvo . . ." His voice trails off, and I suddenly know that after this experience no car will ever just sail through his line again. That he thinks he's lost his ability to judge. And that's shaken him more than the thought of getting AIDS. Albert lowers his sleeve, buttons it. "Let's keep this between you and me, Princess," he adds again.

I make no promises.

The game show is back on and he's watching. "I hope that blonde lady wins," he says. "She sure looks like she could use ten thousand dollars."

How can he even care about her? I wonder. If someone bit me, that's all I'd think about. But not Albert. I can see he really wants her to win.

If there hadn't been a toothpaste commercial, would he have told me about the bite? I know the lady smiling all those white teeth made him remember. I run my tongue over my front teeth and feel the slight overlap. As we watch the woman guess, I find myself circling my thumb and first finger around *my* wrist, which feels as if there isn't any spare skin covering the bone.

Or is he scared and just being brave? The idea of Albert being brave is a new one. It pulls at me all during dinner. He cracks all our crab legs for us, cuts the French bread, and there isn't a trace of fear or self-pity. He just is. Asks Mom about her day and listens to her bitch about how two customers lit up in the no smoking area. Sympathizes when she says her feet are killing her. I can't get the idea of those imprints on his arm out of my mind. I want to say more about the bite but I'm not sure what. I can't believe he can just sit there and eat and not talk about it.

When Mom goes out with the crab shells wrapped tightly in newspaper to the chute in the hall, Albert thunks both elbows on the table, juts his head forward, and scowls at me. It's a pretend scowl — he's trying for my attention. Albert has been known to do

TAKING TOLL

anything for a laugh. Just crossing his eyes makes Mom giggle.

"You're looking at me crabbier than that old crab we just finished," he says. "And he spent his life scuttling sideways underwater before he landed on our supper table."

I don't answer.

"Something bothering you, Princess?" The scowl is gone. He looks directly at me like he wants to help, blinks, and looks away.

"There's this Sports Fair the school's having Saturday," I blurt out. "With fathers." I don't know why I've told him. It was the last thing I planned to do. But there it is standing between us like a huge embarrassment.

He swivels his gaze at me. I expect him to offer to come with me. I expect him to fall all over himself wanting to please — I mean, I know he wants to win me over because of Mom. They've *all* wanted that — at first. The story changes as we go along. That's when their real behavior comes out. I squint at Albert, willing him to say something. *Anything*. But he stays silent as if he's waiting.

"You want to go with me?" I ask, exasperated.

"Sure." His features seem to be melting into each other. Even his eyes are smiling.

"Not that you're my father . . . or anything like that," I add quickly.

"But close enough — for me, at least," he says. "I don't know about you. You see things different from me. You probably would have spotted that Volvo driver as a troublemaker right off." Albert's shyly proud that he's got my attention and he's jammed his right hand in his trouser pocket fiddling with the coins.

"Do you know how to do anything?" I ask him. Something fierce and wild is rushing through me — some terrible kind of feeling I'm not sure of and which is scary. I realize I sound mean, ungrateful, which isn't how I want to sound, but I can't stop. "Use a starting gun? A stopwatch?"

Albert doesn't take offense. He's thoughtful. "I can barbecue good. Most parties I've been to someone needs to know how to barbecue. You could do the games with the other gals and their dads, and I could barbecue everybody's meat."

I don't say anything. I'm already regretting opening my mouth. I have a vivid picture of Albert, wearing his toll taker's uniform, standing beside a smoking barbecue, flipping hot dogs and hamburgers. It's not even that kind of thing. There'll be people to cook. Although I suppose Albert could give them advice. Or he could stand near the finish line and cheer . . . for me.

"So are we on? Do we have a date?" he asks, looking so pleased I can't think of what to say.

He's got a bite on his arm, I remind myself. He could this very minute be dying of AIDS. You could be nice to him just once.

"It's Saturday from eleven-thirty to three. But we don't have to stay more than a couple of hours."

"Unless we're having fun," he says. "Have you seen that bumper sticker, 'Are we having fun yet?'" He goes on to tell me that he's been keeping track of that one. He's counted 523. "I thought it might be fun sometime to run an ad and invite everybody who has *that* bumper sticker on his or her car," he says. "And see what kind of a party that turns out to be."

"This isn't exactly a party," I say. "These are just girls in the ninth grade and their fathers. It's not likely to be much fun. I'd just like to go."

"To be like everybody else," he says, nodding. "I know. I've been there."

Mom comes back, newspaper in hand, complaining that the garbage chute is broken — *again*. Albert gets to his feet and immediately offers to take the crab remains down to a Dumpster he knows about near the liquor store at the corner.

"Isn't he something?" Mom asks when the door shuts behind him.

I don't answer. I can't. Something is lodged in my throat, hard and painful as a baseball. I wonder if I accidentally swallowed a piece of crab shell.

"I don't care what you think about Albert," Mom

snaps. "I love him. And I don't want to hear one nasty word out of your mouth about him. I gave in about the others. But you're wrong about Albert. I love him," she repeats, as if my silence means I've gotten deaf.

I shrug and leave the room, afraid that I'll cry. The last time I cried in front of Mom was when I wanted Jase to go to the Sixth-Grade Fair with me. He said he would. But he went to the races instead. He won. He even offered to split the fifty dollars with me. But I just couldn't forgive him.

I look at the ceiling and think of Albert jingling the coins in his pocket. I think of the teeth marks on his arm. If Albert says he'll go, he'll go. He'd never back out. Not even if he was dying on that very day. I know that, too.

Mom has these set rituals she goes through every night. She takes a shower, sets her hair — even though nobody sets their hair anymore that I know of, Mom does. I wait until I hear the water running. I know I will find Albert out by the TV still dressed, waiting for her to finish. He'll have spread some papers on the coffee table and be polishing his shoes.

I stand quietly in the doorway for a moment. Albert's not watching TV, although it's on. He's not polishing his shoes, either. He's rolled up his sleeve again. He's looking at the bite, pushing at it with his fingers.

"Albert," I say, taking care to keep my voice soft.

He jumps like I've caught him doing something private and quickly rolls down his sleeve. "What is it, Princess?" he asks.

"What did the guy look like?" He knows right off what I mean.

"Like a professor. Wire-rimmed glasses, a beard, his hand was white and very strong."

"He sounds like someone who was fired. I think he was just mad. You asked him for money and he flipped out. I'm sure he didn't have AIDS."

"Why thank you, Miranda," Albert says slowly.

For some reason I can't just drop it. "But maybe you should be tested . . . just to be sure."

"I'll do that," he says after a second. "Okay?" He doesn't tell me to stop worrying, but I know that's what he means. His face has turned into one giant question mark. Albert doesn't like anybody to worry.

"Okay," I answer. I think it's the first time I've ever answered Albert directly. But he doesn't seem to notice. All along he's pretended that I answer. He just expects what you've said or haven't said and responds. Kind of like saying, "Thank you," I guess, sometimes over four thousand times a day, to everyone who hands him a dollar to cross the bridge.

Building Bridges

At first, Mama Lil said it plain and simple: "No." Then, like always, she spoke her full mind. "Bebe, get that backward idea out your head. That grit-work ain't no place for you. And besides, I ain't never heard of no girls to be doing *that*. You need to be getting yourself a real summer job, something civilized."

We'd just finished Sunday breakfast. Mama Lil had fried up a batch of Dunbar's ham, the meat we ate only on Sundays, holidays, and special occasions — my all-time favorite.

Mama Lil pushed her breakfast plate aside and centered her ashtray. She took a final drag on her cigarette. Through the haze of smoke that clouded her small, tight face, she spoke slow and deliberate. "And don't ask me again about signing that permission paper," she said. "I ain't gonna be the one who allows you to take part in such foolishness."

I leaned back in my kitchen chair, my arms folded tight. The chair's vinyl stuck to the skin on my shoulders, taping itself to the place where my T-shirt scooped down at my back. It was as if, like Mama Lil, that chair wanted to hold me in its clutches.

I'd been living with Mama Lil since I was six, when my own mama and daddy were taken by the Walcott apartment building fire. Lillian Jones was my mom's mother. Everybody on our street called my grandmother Mama Lil, and that's what I called her, too. She was a mama to everybody, it seemed, always scolding the other neighborhood kids about playing their music too loudly in the street, or hanging out too long on the front stoop of our house. Mama Lil and I had been butting heads ever since I could remember. And the older I got, the more at odds we were.

Mama Lil hated the six studs I wore in my left ear; I hated the tacky red wig she pulled down close to her eyebrows whenever her hair wasn't done.

She thought I weighed too much and dressed badly; I thought she smoked too much and overdid it with her fake gold chains. Time after time, she'd asked me, "How you ever gonna land a decent man with them chunky arms and those hoochie-cut T-shirts that put your navel on parade? No self-respecting

ANDREA DAVIS PINKNEY

seventeen-year-old should be letting it all hang out like *that*."

Whenever Mama Lil got on her "self-respecting seventeen-year-old" sermon, I came back with a warning under my breath: "When some homey *tries* to snatch all that shiny tin off your seventy-three-year-old neck, don't come crying to me."

If Mama Lil really wanted to heap it on, she'd start nagging me about my hair. "Child," she liked to say, "them natty braids you call dreadlocks look like the fright 'do of a zombie."

Yeah, over the years Mama Lil and I had thrown a lot of dissing words back and forth. But then, too, I had a sister-to-sister connection to Mama Lil that not many kids had with their grandmas. I could talk to her real direct. I could tell her the deal, straight up.

Mama Lil and I didn't beat around the bush because all we had was each other. There was no time to waste on half-spoken words. I was Mama Lil's only true family, and she was the only real parent I had. If I ever left her, she'd have nobody; and if she passed on, I'd be alone in this world.

For weeks I'd been asking Mama Lil to let me join the youth renovation team, a group of kids that had been chosen by city officials to work with a squad of contract engineers to help repair the Brooklyn Bridge. The project would last the summer, pay good money, and help me get to college, where I wanted to study engineering. The whole thing sure beat flipping Big Macs at Mickey Dee's.

But Mama Lil wasn't having it. To her, I was "stooping to do a bunch of low-down mess-work." Truth be told, Mama Lil was scared of something she didn't know. She hardly ever left our neighborhood in Brooklyn; to her, the Brooklyn Bridge was a mystery.

And I think that deep down Mama Lil was afraid something bad would happen to me, the same way it happened to my mama and daddy. Also, Mama Lil couldn't read or write very well — I read most of her mail to her, and helped her sign her checks — and she hated to admit it. The two-page consent form she had to sign, giving me permission to work on the bridge project, was a challenge to her pride.

Then there was the fact that I would be the only girl working with the bridge crew. (My acceptance letter said few girls had applied; of those who did, I was the only qualified candidate, based on my grades.) Mama Lil thought it just wasn't right that I'd be working on a project staffed only with boys and men. "If God had meant you to do a man's work, he would have made you a man. It's that simple," she said.

All these strikes stood against me ever getting to work on that bridge. But the biggest obstacle of all, the thing that made Mama Lil the most stubborn, was my dream of becoming an engineer. Mama Lil didn't fully understand what an engineer was. I'd tried to explain it to her; I'd shown her my sketchbook full of drawings of city structures and machines, but Mama Lil didn't *know* any engineers. She'd never seen one at work.

And to make matters worse, she'd taken it upon herself to ask her friends down at Rimley's Beauty Parlor about engineering. They'd convinced her that I was headed down the wrong path. "Ain't no black woman doing no engine-ing," she'd said.

"Engin*eering*," I'd corrected.

Mama Lil said, "Whatever you call it, it's a white man's work. You ain't got no place messing with it. We should stick with our own kind, Bebe — colored women trying to cross the white man's line is asking for trouble."

In some respects, Mama Lil was right. Black folks did need to stick together, no doubt. But not in the way Mama Lil meant. And it *was* true that there weren't many black women engineers. I knew from the get-go that if I hoped to become an engineer, my road ahead would be lonely and hard. But I wanted to build bridges more than anything. And working on the bridge project was the first step — a step that I needed Mama Lil's help to make. A step that started right here in her tiny kitchen.

The last of Mama Lil's cigarette smoke lingered between us.

"I wish you'd lay off those Carltons," I said, pushing the smoke away with a single wave of my hand.

Mama Lil rose from the table. She took her ashtray with her. "I'm trying to quit, Bebe, you know that," she said. "Carltons have less tar, less nicotine. They're better for you," she reasoned.

"And I'm Miss America," I huffed.

At the sink, Mama Lil lit another cigarette, then started washing the dishes. "Look, missy," she scolded, "don't be taking your bad mood out on me. You get cranky every time we talk about that nasty job you want to get." Mama Lil turned her back to me and began to fill the sink with soapy water.

"It's *not* nasty," I said, my voice rising. "Hooking and turning tricks is nasty. Selling to the crackheads is nasty. But this is good work, Mama Lil. I'd be employed by the city — by the mayor."

Mama Lil was busy lathering the greasy skillet she'd used to fry the ham. With her back to me — she had strong back muscles that showed beneath her blouse — she said, "Bebe, I don't care if you're working for the King of Siam. Hammering a bridge together is not respectable work for a young lady."

"But, Mama Lil, working on the bridge isn't just —"

"— Don't get me wrong, Bebe" — Mama Lil kept her back to me — "all those pretty pictures you draw in that tablet of yours are real nice. But, child, doing that to earn a living is a pipe dream. *White* folks can pay their bills by sitting around doodling. We just don't got it like that."

I leaned my forehead onto the heels of both my hands. The kitchen hung quiet for a moment, its only sound the scrub of Brillo scratching the ham skillet. Mama Lil cleaned in a steady, determined rhythm. With each scrub, she hunched further over the sink, giving that pan every bit of strength she had. "This damn grease is stubborn," she said, her back muscles tense with effort.

"*You're* stubborn," I spat in a low voice. But Mama Lil didn't hear me. She just kept on scrubbing.

That evening Mama Lil dozed off in front of her little black-and-white television set. The blue cast of the TV's light danced across her face, softening its tired lines. Mama Lil wheezed out small, breathy snores. She was sinking into the kind of sleep that often kept her on the couch — TV babbling on — all night.

I locked Mama Lil safe inside the house, and, with my sketchbook tucked firm under my arm, I headed for the street. As I walked our noisy avenue, I took in the lights and people who dotted the darkness. I thought hard about Mama Lil's mule-headed words: "Ain't no black woman doing no engineering . . . trying to cross the white man's line is asking for trouble."

I walked fast and furious for blocks and blocks, the warm summer air heaving in my lungs. My armpits had grown sticky with perspiration. The hair at my temples began to crimp with sweat. Finally, I stopped under a streetlight — a streetlight that was my hiding place — on a quiet corner, just off Shore Street. I leaned into the streetlight's cold aluminum pole, letting my breath slow itself down.

Ahead, in the distance, stood the Brooklyn Bridge. This was the best spot in Brooklyn's Red Hook section for seeing the bridge. I'd come to this corner and studied the bridge a million times. And on every one of those times, I was taken with what I'd come to call Brooklyn Belle.

I never got tired of looking out at its steel girders and iron cables — at its beautiful crisscross rafters that had started out in somebody's imagination, had been put to paper, formalized in an engineer's plans, then woven together, bolt by bolt. Now Belle was a powerful giant who carried all kinds of people to all kinds of places, day after day.

At night Belle was dressed in tiny lights that spanned her limbs. On a cloudless night like this one, she was a sight like no other sight in the whole city. Jeweled in light. *Beautiful.*

My fingers had tensed into fists at my sides, fists full of strength and eagerness. I uncurled my knuckles and shook them free of their strain. Then I reached into my jacket pocket — where my consent form for the bridge project had been neatly folded for days — and pulled out my pencil. Slowly, I flipped through the pages of my sketchbook. I'd drawn Belle in the high-noon light, at sunset, on snowy days, and on foggy twilight mornings. My favorite sketches were those of Belle during rush hour, when cars and taxis danced like trinkets along her outstretched beams.

Tonight I'd draw Belle with her lighted cape. I sketched slowly at first, then faster, my pencil working with the speed of my excitement — the thrill that worked me over every time I sketched that bridge.

I was proud of my drawings (I liked to think of them as portraits), but with each page they showed a sad truth about Belle: She needed repair. She was some forty years older than Mama Lil. And as lovely as she was, she had some serious rough spots — corroded cables, rust, chipped paint, and plain old grit that had built up over the decades. That bridge renovation project needed me; and I needed it, in more ways than I could count.

The air had grown sticky, moistening the pages of

my sketchbook. It was getting late. The orange glow of the streetlight above my head flickered in the blue-black night. I slid my pencil back to its pocket, and headed for home.

If I'd had a bet on it, I'd have put my money down that Mama Lil hadn't missed me one bit. She was probably snoring up a storm by now. And her TV was most likely still blipping its hues onto her face, sending its random talk-show chatter around her living room.

A week passed. A week of Mama Lil and I not speaking about the bridge project, or the permission form that was due — signed by her — in four days, when the renovation was supposed to begin.

We talked about plenty of other things — the hell-hot summer heat, the tomatoes at Key Food, Oprah's new look — but we sidestepped talk about the bridge altogether. And with each avoidance, with each conversation about nothing at all, the Brooklyn Bridge loomed larger. It was as if Belle were sitting smack center in Mama Lil's living room, with grid-locked traffic fighting for space on her pavement. If I didn't get my consent form signed, I would forfeit my place on the project. Every time I tried to bring it up, Mama Lil twisted her lips and raised her hand. "Don't be bringing that mess in here, Bebe. There ain't no more discussing to do."

As the days passed, I grew more anxious, and

ANDREA DAVIS PINKNEY

more angry at Mama Lil's attitude. On the Saturday night before the project was to start, Mama Lil did something that got me real mad. She brought home a summer job application from Rimley's Beauty Parlor, where she and her gossipy friends spent their days.

As Mama Lil lifted the application from her purse, she had the nerve to say, "Bebe, I went and done you a big favor." I gave Mama Lil a hard sideways stare.

She kept on talking. "Vernice Rimley needs somebody to sweep hair and clean her sinks. She can't pay you nothing to start, but you'd get a heap of training. By next summer you'd be doing perms and manicures, and getting tips on top of a regular salary. And you could even bring your paper tablet, so you can draw during your breaks."

Mama Lil put the application down on the coffee table between us. As she spoke, she tapped it with her finger, emphasizing her words. "Bebe, if you put your mind to it, you could be awfully good at doing hair. Give it a chance, child," she urged.

My forehead and upper lip grew moist with the sweat that anger brings on. I wiped the back of my hand across my mouth, feeling my words jump to my throat before I spoke them.

Mama Lil lit a Carlton. She sat back on her sofa, blowing smoke straight ahead. Her eyes avoided mine. "Mama Lil," I began, "*look* at me."

But Mama Lil was sinking deeper into her stubbornness. She leaned her head back, inhaled on her cigarette, and closed her eyes to release another stream of smoke. "I'm enjoying my cig, Bebe," she said. "It tastes better with my eyes closed."

I leaned in the doorway, my anger rising. "Mama Lil, your eyes are *always* closed. *Closed* to seeing me." Mama Lil's lips curled around the tip of her Carlton, letting the cigarette dangle for a moment.

I said, "I don't want to spend my summer sweeping hair. The bridge is where my heart's at, Mama Lil."

Mama Lil shifted on her couch pillow. I could see her eyes roaming beneath their lids. She took another drag, a heavy one this time, and blew out a long, quick breath. She was doing her best to tune me out. "Yeah, that's right," I said, my voice strained with frustration, "blow me away. Try to make me and my dreams disappear, like your puffs of smoke!" I was hollering now, full out. I kicked the doorjamb with the toe of my sneaker. "Damn!"

Mama Lil opened her eyes in search of the cat-shaped ashtray she kept on her coffee table. She tapped her ashes into the cat's face, then aligned her gaze with mine. Her eyes looked weary, her expression pained. She set her Carlton along the cat's ceramic tail and let it smolder. She sighed. "Bebe, I'm an old woman. I ain't got much to look forward to in this life — not many of my own dreams to go after." Mama Lil's voice trailed off to silence. Then her face softened, and for the first time ever, I saw Mama Lil's eyes fill with regret. "What little bit of dreaming I got left in me," she said, "I'm putting to you."

I licked my lips and listened. Mama Lil had more to say. "But I can't dream your dreams, Bebe. Working on that old bridge so that you can study some high-tone thing like engineering is a far-off notion that don't fit in this old woman's way."

Mama Lil let out a heavy breath. Then she admitted what we'd both known all along. "Your dreams are the kind that'll take you away from here, Bebe — away from your Mama Lil. You got big hopes, child, but they gonna leave me alone, by myself."

I shrugged.

Mama Lil said, "That's an upsetting truth, Bebe. It makes my heart hurt every time I think on it." The cigarette had burned to ash. Its smoke had gone, but its heavy odor remained in the room.

Mama Lil was right. My dreams *would* take me away from her.

I wanted to comfort her, but I wasn't willing to back out of the bridge project, or give up my plans for becoming an engineer. I knelt next to the couch cushion where Mama Lil sat and took both her hands in mine.

"Mama Lil, I got to find *my* way," I said slowly. "If that bridge renovation wasn't tapping on my soul, I'd go ahead and sweep hair down at Rimley's."

For once, Mama Lil was looking into my face, hearing my words. Her eyes were filled with sad acknowledgment.

"Let me go, Mama Lil. Let me dream," I pleaded softly.

Mama Lil sat as still as a statue. I gently pulled my hands away from hers and reached into my pocket to find the bridge project consent form. I unfolded the thick carboned papers and set them on the coffee table, next to the application from Rimley's. "Mama Lil," I said carefully, "if you don't sign this — if you *won't* sign it — I'll sign it myself. I been helping you sign checks and letters for years now. I can sign your name on this consent form, and nobody'll know the difference."

Mama Lil's eyes began to dart. She looked from me to the consent form to the Rimley's application, and back to me again.

"I don't want to cross you, Mama Lil," I said, "but I will if I have to — to do what makes my soul feel right. To dream my dreams."

Mama Lil reached for her pack of Carltons, which were resting on the arm of her sofa. She felt for a cigarette, but the package was empty. I smoothed the consent form with my palm. "You want me to read you what it says?" I asked.

Mama Lil shook her head. "Leave it be," she insisted. "Let me sit with it awhile."

I could feel my face growing warm again with perspiration. Night had fallen fully now, but Mama Lil's cramped living room still sweltered from the daytime heat. I could hear the boys on our block gathering to play their music on the corner. Usually Mama Lil would call from the window, hassling them to "turn that blasted noise down." But all she said was, "Bebe, get on to bed. It's getting late." I rose to my feet, hovering over Mama Lil, who, for the first time ever, looked small and sunken in her seat. "The bridge project starts tomorrow morning," I reminded her.

Mama Lil shrugged. "I know good and well when it starts, Bebe. You've told me twenty times over."

That night, the night before I was to report to the bridge project, I lay awake. I was afraid Mama Lil would doze off in front of her TV and forget about the consent form. Or that the detailed instructions on the two-page sheet would frustrate her, and she wouldn't make the effort to read it through. And worse than that, I feared Mama Lil would set fire to the form with her cigarette lighter.

When I finally fell asleep, all kinds of strange dreams danced in my head: Mama Lil crossing a bridge made of Carlton cigarettes; my sketchbook filling itself with senseless scribbles; the hair from the floor of Rimley's Beauty Parlor floating up and clinging to my face, making it hard for me to breathe.

I awoke to the smell of Dunbar's ham coming from the kitchen. The sun hadn't risen; twilight slowly approached. I listened for Mama Lil's TV, but all I heard was crackling grease and the shuffle of Mama Lil's feet against the kitchen tile.

My clock said 5:36. The bridge renovation crew was scheduled to meet at 7:00 at the Tillary Street entrance to the bridge. I threw on my muscle T-shirt and jeans and grabbed my sketchbook.

When I got to the kitchen, my place was set. Mama Lil scurried between the stove and the table, setting down napkins, pouring orange juice, flipping the ham as it rustled in the skillet. She didn't even see me come into the kitchen. "Hey, Mama Lil," I said.

Mama Lil peered at me over the top of her narrow glasses, glasses she wore only for reading. Glasses that hung from the chain of one of her junk jewelry necklaces. "Sit, Bebe, your ham's ready," she said. I shrugged and slid into my chair. The sun was full in the sky, zigzagging its light across the kitchen table. The hands on the kitchen clock were settling on 6:00.

Mama Lil served both our plates. She sat down across from me and started eating. She was acting like it was any other morning, chatting on about her late-night comedy show and the pigeons that nested on the ledge of her bedroom window. I was certain she'd done away with the consent form for the bridge project, and was doing her best to ignore the whole thing.

I ate in silence, wondering if the bridge crew leader would let me onto the project without signed permission. I'd have to leave for the site soon, if I wanted to get there on time.

Mama Lil hadn't stopped talking. Now she was on to something about the high price of cornmeal.

I finished my last bite of ham, and interrupted. "Mama Lil," I said firmly, "I'm going to the bridge."

Mama Lil steadied her glasses. She took a heavy breath. "I know, Bebe," she said, nodding, "I know."

That's when Mama Lil reached into the pocket of her housedress and pulled out the consent form. "You gonna need this," she said, sliding the papers across the table.

I unfolded the form, which had become worn and crumpled. But Mama Lil hadn't signed it. It was the same as it had always been.

Mama Lil could see the upset pinching at my face. "Now hold it, Bebe," she said, "don't be so quick to put on that down-in-the-mouth expression."

"But you didn't sign the form, Mama Lil, and you know I can't —"

"Calm down, child." Mama Lil's tone was solid. She said, "You're jumping out the gate too fast."

"The project's gonna start without me!" I snapped.

Mama Lil leaned into the table toward me. Her eyes looked red-tired. Before I could speak another heated word, Mama Lil said, "I been up most the night, Bebe — thinking, praying, and trying my best to read that confounded permission paper. They sure got a whole bunch of words typed on that thing, just to say I'm gonna let you help fix a bridge."

I could feel my whole body fill with relief. Mama Lil said, "I may not know how to read that good, but I *do* know I ain't supposed to sign something I ain't fully read."

Mama Lil pushed her glasses up further on her nose. They were speckled with dots of grease that had sprung from the hot ham skillet. "Will you help me read the permission paper, Bebe?" she asked. "Will you help me understand what it's saying to me?"

I slid my chair to Mama Lil's side of the table. Together, we read the consent form, line by line. When we were done, Mama Lil took a pen from her house-dress pocket. She held it awkwardly and signed the form with her crooked handwriting.

She gave her signature a good looking-over. Her face filled with satisfaction. Then she folded the form and pressed it into my hand. "Bebe, that bridge is lucky to have you," she said.

I hugged Mama Lil good and hard, then I got up to go. Just before I left the kitchen, I turned and smiled big, right at her. "Yeah, it is," I said.

Guess Who's Back in Town, Dear?

Prom Night. After Drew got sick, he sat in his new white sports car with the door open. He sat where he'd never sat, and would likely never sit again: opposite the driver's seat.

"Are you okay now?" Tory asked him.

Drew couldn't answer her right away. He was holding his head up with one hand, his hair falling over his face. He was blond and green-eyed like Tory. People said they looked enough alike to be brother and sister.

She had never seen Drew drunk. She knew he'd gone into the boys' john with some of the seniors so he wouldn't come across as a stuck-up preppie, too good for his old crowd.

"I have to go home, Tor. I'm really sorry."

"That's all right."

"No, it is not all right, and I'm sorry."

She waited to see if he'd get behind the wheel. She wondered if he remembered that she didn't know how to operate a stick shift.

She stood there in her new long white gown. There was no way she could go to the after-prom party alone, even though Drew had paid the hundred-dollar-a-couple charge for the band and breakfast. No one went alone.

The highlight of the prom was the Elvis impersonator. Tory could hear him from the parking lot. He was singing "It's Now or Never." He was good, too.

Drew was holding his face with both hands.

Tory looked down at the red carnation that had fallen to the gravel from his lapel. She thought of painting what she saw and calling it "Prom Night." She picked up the flower and held it.

"Do you need some help, Miss Victoria King?"

He was the one who'd worn a pink dinner jacket to the dance. Drew had nicknamed him "The Flamingo." His real name had been forgotten by most everyone, since he'd come to school in the middle of senior year.

He had black curly hair and brown eyes, was medium height and on the skinny side.

Tory said, "I don't think we've really met, have we?"

"My mother works for your mother."

M. E. KERR

"You mean Maria?" She was the Kings' new maid.

He nodded. "I'm Horacio Vargas. How can I help here?"

Luckily, he'd come to the prom stag.

He drove Tory home first.

He was from New York City, he said, and someday he was going to write a novel. But first he would become a lawyer. He already knew a lot about law, and he read all the time.

When he asked her what she was planning to do, she said she was going to Vassar, and so was Drew.

"To become what?"

"College graduates," she laughed. But when he didn't seem to think her answer was all that funny, she said, "Drew will go into real estate with my dad. He'll buy houses, and I'll fix them up to sell . . . maybe."

"Maybe?"

"We'll see. . . . We're coming back here to live."

"You sounded like there was more. You said 'maybe' as if you had a secret wish."

"We'll come back and live up on the lake. We both love the lake."

Drew was curled up in a fetal position in the small space behind them.

"This city gives me the shivers, though," said Horacio.

"Because of the prison?" Arcade was known for that.

"There it is to remind you how you can go so wrong."

Horacio hitchhiked home that night after he helped Drew's father carry him inside.

He put the carnation she'd given him inside his Bible.

After he told his mother what had happened, he added, "If I had such a girl for my date, I wouldn't be passing the bottle in the boys' toilet."

"Victoria King ruined your prom night," his mom said. "You didn't rent that beautiful jacket to be a chauffeur!"

"What about her night?"

"Worry about yourself, Horacio, not them. They won't ever worry about you, you can count on that."

Mr. Victor King, a prominent Arcade realtor, enjoys telling the following about a certain New Year's Eve in New York City.

Invited there by a client, he and Mrs. King were not unpleasantly surprised when it was explained that after dinner everyone was heading in limos to Grand Central Station, to hand out sandwiches to the homeless.

Mrs. King was secretly apprehensive that one of

them might call her names or indulge in threatening behavior.

"Not to worry, Mrs. Best Friend," Mr. King reassured, using his pet name for her. "The mayor himself is going to be there. You'll be well protected."

Mr. King borrowed an old baseball cap from his host and put on his Nike running clothes, which he took everywhere with him since his cholesterol had gone over 300.

At Grand Central, he set off to hand out salami heroes in the tunnels around the subways, while Mrs. King joined the ladies at the tables in the main waiting room.

The thing is — on Victor King's way back, as he was walking along by himself, someone tried to give *him* a sandwich!

Victor King always cracks up telling the story, and when he gets control again, he says, "I had to tell the fellow, thanks, but *I'm* one of *you!*"

"Thanks for the other night," Tory said.

She'd gone purposely to the A & P to find him, after Maria'd told her that was where he worked.

Drew parked outside, waiting for her, another couple in the back of his car. They were all old friends who'd been sailing their Stars and Comets alongside one another and swimming at the club together since they were little.

Drew had given Tory an envelope with a fifty-dollar bill inside.

"Is this money?" Horacio said, not waiting for an answer. He shook his head and handed back the envelope.

"It's not from me, Horatio. It's from Drew."

"Hor-*rass*-cio. No 't.' No money, either. It was a favor to you."

He had on a long white apron, and he was carrying a mop. He was cleaning up after someone who'd dropped a jar of pickles on the cement floor.

"But how can I ever return the favor?" Tory asked him. "It's not fair to make me indebted to you, Horacio."

His shirtsleeves were rolled. There was a silver identification bracelet clanking against his Timex.

Drew never wore jewelry, not even a class ring.

Neither did Tory's father.

Both of them agreed rings were not right for men, not even wedding rings.

"I like books," Horacio said. "You can buy me a paperback. You can buy me any paperback by Gabriel García Márquez."

Tory wrote down the name, since she had never heard of that author.

"A gift for the maid's boy?" Mrs. King said, amazed.

"I told you about it. You never listen."

"I listen. It's a little extreme, darling. Do you know why Maria moved to Arcade?"

"I suppose you're going to say she's some prisoner's relative."

"I'm afraid I am. . . . Her husband is in Arcade Prison."

Tory remembered her father's harangues about the "riffraff" moving right into Arcade, instead of just visiting their jailbird relatives. Mr. King often said he didn't mind paying taxes for schools and roads and hospitals, but he *did* mind shelling out for welfare for the "junkies' families."

"Those are junkies inside those walls. They're not like our old convicts," he'd say, as though he had fond memories of thieves and murderers from bygone days.

"Maria works hard," Mrs. King told Tory while Tory tied a red ribbon around the package for Horacio. "But her husband got in there because of drugs, so I thought I'd just not mention anything. You know how your father hates addicts."

"What about some of his friends up at the country club? You could pour them out of there weekends."

"Oh, that's apples and oranges you're trying to compare, Tory. Why, you even drew one of your little sketches on the wrapping paper, and is that a note you're enclosing?"

"It's just a thank-you note, Mother . . . and yes, I did one of my little sketches on the paper." Tory hated that certain condescending tone her mother would get at times.

This is the note Tory'd written to Horacio:

I read a little of this and I love it, so I bought a copy for myself, too.

Thanks for telling me about this author, Horacio.

Next time I see you we can discuss Love in the Time of Cholera. *I do have a secret wish. It is to be a painter.*

She'd signed her name *Victoria,* though no one called her that except for him, that first time on prom night.

Another story Mr. King enjoys telling always begins with the time he called upstairs to his wife, "Laura? Guess who's back in town, dear?"

He often retells it when they're out dining with their special crowd, all long-time Arcadians, all with clear memories of Richard Lasher.

Only teachers called him by his first name.

He was a troublemaker from the start, so good-looking more than one Arcadian said some talent

M. E. KERR

42 STAY TRUE

scout ought to see him. Let Hollywood deal with Lasher!

Mrs. King thought he was like some wild and beautiful weed appearing suddenly on a grand green lawn.

He'd come to Arcade because of the prison, too.

But he'd come as the new warden's son.

Everyone said it was a good thing he knew his way around the prison. He'd have no trouble finding things when he got sent there.

One time he was picked up for shoplifting in the A & P and another time he drove off in someone's car on County Fair Day. He'd crawl into the Schine Cinema window from the fire escape, or he'd break into the YMCA after midnight for a skinny dip. He set a pig loose down a church aisle on a Sunday and he stole the iron balls from the Civil War memorial cannon on the village green.

Then when he grew up, it was girls. It was fathers keeping guard over their daughters, for fear he'd break one of their hearts or worse. Mostly it was "or worse" they worried about when it came to Lasher.

He was charming, devilish, a looker, and he had his own car. A van.

A *big* van, decorated hippy style, stereo inside and heaven knows what else.

And then . . . and everyone in Arcade remembered it — it was Lasher and Laura Waite.

"Before my time," Mr. King likes to say, with that cocky smile of his.

Mrs. King gets red, always. It is a story she doesn't think he should tell, not because she cares that Lasher has become a prison guard in Florida and a Born-Again. "Bald now, and *fat*? He breaks chairs. Swear it!" Mr. King often has to stop laughing before he can continue. "I didn't know who he was, he's so bloated."

For Mrs. King this particular story is not about what Lasher has become, as much as it is about what passion does to love when passion has a say in it.

Who didn't know what was going on between them? Who'd never seen the two of them together, how they couldn't keep their hands off each other, couldn't stop grinning and looking into each other's eyes?

Victor King continues: "Says, 'How's my Laura?' to me. *His* Laura!" Mr. King slaps his knee.

No, it is not what Lasher turned out to be that makes Mrs. King embarrassed for her husband.

No one can take back the fact that Laura Waite *was* Lasher's girl. Mrs. King thinks of it as ages and ages ago, the year she wrote the poem.

Her mother found it at the back of Laura's diary and demanded an explanation.

Laura said, "Why don't *you* explain why you snooped?"

"Lips your lips on mine," her mother read sourly, *"And wet your eyes, eyes, eyes,/Not yet, not yet.* What does that mean?"

But Mrs. Waite knew the answer to that question. That fall Laura found herself attending Miss Grey's for Girls, off in Pennsylvania.

In all her life she'd only written the one poem.

"What did you like about it?" Horacio asked.

Tory'd been passing by, somehow, just as the supermarket was closing for the night.

"That the hero was so intense, I think," said Tory. "And that it was really much more than just a love story."

"You know the author, García Márquez? I was born in the town where he was born. Aracataca, Colombia."

He took her hand then, just like that. Of course, they had come to a crossing, but he was going to hold it after they got to the other side. She knew it.

He said, "All that intensity is my birthright." He looked at her to test how her eyes would take that and he saw them shining back. Now he was almost sure of what he'd dared to hope when he first saw her lingering outside.

A night of firecrackers and stars.

They sat in the canvas chairs along the front lawn

of the club, facing the lake. Drew had on white pants and a red T-shirt, long and lean in this, the last summer of their youth.

Tory had called it that a moment ago, holding a sparkler away from her yellow halter dress. Drew stretched his legs out in front of him and said that he expected his youth to last until the end of college.

"But it's the last time we'll be living with our parents, full-time. Did you ever think of that?"

"This will always be home," Drew said. "Did I tell you what dad's giving us for a wedding present? Four of the ten acres he owns up on the lake. Neat, huh?"

"That's four years away," Tory said.

The Fourth of July was at full pitch, loud and spectacular in the sky above them.

"Dad's not developing his six acres, either. He and Mother will build on three and save three for the grandkids. We'll have our own compound."

"Do you love me, Drew?"

"No," he said, "I'm marrying you out of habit."

"That's not funny."

"Of course I love you. Who do I love if I don't love you?"

"Who do I love," she said, "if I don't love you?"

"Exactly," he said.

"No, not exactly." She started to tell him. . . . She was going to begin by asking him if he was ever curious what she did those evenings he spent watching sports on TV or going to ball games.

She tried to think of another way to start off, a way that would not put him on the defensive. Nothing he had done had anything to do with Horacio.

She was almost ready to do it, but in the pause he said, "That land's worth about thirty thousand an acre. In four more years, it'll be worth a lot more. We've really got it made, Tory!"

Rockets burst overhead and behind them the band began to play "Oh, Susannah."

One day a white rose was waiting for Tory when she came back from the club.

So was her mother.

"I'm sorry," Mrs. King said, "but the card fell out of the tissue paper, and I read it."

The card said, *The last line of LITOC from your H.*

LITOC stood for the novel by García Márquez.

"Well?" said Mrs. King. "What does it mean?"

"I'll have to look it up," said Tory, who'd never have to look it up to remember it.

"You know what I'm asking you. What is this all about, dear? He calls himself '*Your* H.'?"

"When you were in love with that Lasher, what was it all about?" Tory asked.

"Tory, Richard Lasher was the son of the warden.

He wasn't the son of someone inside. He was of our own kind, not an ethnic. He went to middle school and high school here, and we all knew the family."

"I didn't ask you what Lasher was about. I asked you what *it* was about."

Mrs. King drew a deep breath.

She sat down on her daughter's bed.

She said finally, "When did all this happen?"

"If you get her in trouble, your life will be ruined," said Maria Vegas.

"I don't touch her."

"Sure, and I'm that blonde Madonna from the MTV."

"I don't. We're going away, Mama."

"What does your father say?"

"To go. To marry her."

"He said that?"

"He said when he fell in love and married it was the best thing of his life."

His mother blushed and bit away a little smile. "There's more to come," she said. "It's not over, tell him."

"And he thanked me for bringing her there to meet him, for asking him his opinion."

"What did he think, you'd leave your own father out?"

While she waits for him to come home this night, Mrs. King is thinking of things she has gone over and over in her head all day.

She thinks of the greeting card he always presents to her three times a year: on Valentine's Day, on their anniversary, and on her birthday. She finds one propped up against the water glass at her place, at the breakfast table. He is already at work by then, since they never eat together in the morning, and she immediately thanks him, telephoning his office to do so.

The cards are the big, mushy sort with words on them he would never dream of speaking.

She thinks, too, of his habit of telling her he feels like scratching an itch. It has become his way of saying that he's what Tory would call horny. Mrs. King hates that word, as well. Mrs. King thinks of it as wanting to make love, though that is not the most accurate description of what actually happens.

And Mrs. King remembers how surprised she used to be when she was with her girlfriends and they would admit to similar things going on in their lives. All of them did; all admitted it and laughed.

There was a warm camaraderie in the laughter, as though they all belonged to the same sorority . . . and one of them might say with a certain affectionate indignation, "Men!"

When she hears his car drive up, she steels herself.

She tries to remember what Tory said to tell him: Vassar isn't the only college — New York City has several very fine ones, including Parsons School of Design, and Cooper Union, for artists. Tory does not expect any help from home, either. Both she and Horacio are going to find jobs in New York.

And Mrs. King is to try and make him understand that since Horacio came into her life, Tory realizes she did not love Drew that way at all. She was never in love with him. Drew was more like a best friend. No . . . Mrs. King decides to omit that description of Drew.

Wham! — the slam of the Chrysler's door, and now he is on his way up the walk.

Mrs. King's heart is racing with an excitement she has not felt for ages and ages.

They had composed their own marriage vows.

They were very simple ones, ending with Tory saying, "We, Victoria and Horacio, will love each other forever."

A pause for the exchange of rings.

Then it was Horacio's turn. "'Forever, he said,'" which is the last line of *Love in the Time of Cholera*.

Going Fishing

The alarm is set for four A.M., but before it goes off, Grace opens her eyes. The happiness of a dream is still on her. She sees the sign taped to her bedside table written in luminescent purple: GET OUTTA BED. NOW. THIS MEANS YOU, DARLING. Her little looove note to herself. Her clothes are laid out; her fishing gear is waiting downstairs; all she has to do is kick out of bed, and in less than an hour she'll park her father's car near the abandoned quarry, cross the road, and scramble down the bank with her pole and tackle box.

Through the drawn shade, she sees the sun coming up red and hazy. She thinks of casting out her line and watching it break through the glassy sheen of the reservoir, and her heart actually beats harder. But the room is dim and the bed deliciously warm. Maybe she could sleep for five more minutes, sleep and dream about A.B. . . .

Suddenly she lets out a squawk, remembering the actual dream she had just before she woke up. Damn. She had dreamed about Vronsky. She almost squawks again, but glancing over at her sister, she holds it back. Faith's hell on wheels if you wake her up. Did she really dream about Richard Vronsky, history teacher with an attitude? Whom she detests.

Actually, Mr. Vronsky doesn't have an attitude, he has an attitude's attitude. He doesn't walk, he struts. He doesn't speak, he proclaims. He probably looks in the mirror every morning and says, *I am a Superior Being*. Plus, he has a military haircut, short spikes of dirty blond hair. Plus, she truly hates the way he shaves.

Not, of course, that she's ever seen him in the act of shaving, but every morning in class she is forced to gaze at his raw-skinned visage, his square jaw flecked with blood, and little bits of bloody tissue clinging to the skin of his neck. Worst of all, though, she is forced to listen to him. "Miss Trembly," he says to her friend Jane, with exaggerated, ironic courtesy, "please give us the benefit of your profound thoughts on this question." Sometimes he calls Jane Madame Editor in the same sarcastic tone. Jane's an editor of the school paper, but so is Boyd Wheeler, and Vronsky never, ever, speaks to Boyd like that.

"Madame Editor, as a person with an informed view of the world . . ." That's how Vronsky talks, when he talks to a female at all. Jane, because she's important in school. Shannon Li, because she's spectacularly pretty. But to Grace, never. She should be glad not to be noticed by such a dismal specimen of maleness, but the fact is that it makes her furious. She has plenty to say about everything, but never gets a chance in Vronsky's class. How depressing that she dreamed of him! Why not dream about someone she relishes, someone she admires or at least finds good-looking enough to be a sex object? Why not dream about A. B.?

But when she's the way she is now — in what she calls *a state of longing* — when the sweet misery rises in her body and at night she curls on herself tenderly; when, all day, she looks at every male creature and wonders when one will ever look back at her and see her the way she wants to be seen; when she cries in the shower for no reason and sometimes even reverts to her old childish habit of hiding in the closet, her face buried and swollen among the clothes; when she's this way, then there is no knowing what her wilful, her unpredictable, her uncontrollable unconscious will do to her. What dreams it will shower down on her. What little tricks it will pull.

The little trick, this time, was to please her with one of those sweet and stinging dreams in which she is wanted, held, noticed, known. In which all that she feels is given back. Given back by the detestable Mr. V.? Some people believe in dreams as predictors of reality. She could never hold to that view. She knows the difference between daylight and dreams. But, to tell the truth, she's had dreams like this before, the kind in which things happen that her conscious mind knows are absurd. And not only night dreams. Daydreams, too.

The night dreams, of course, are beyond her control; the daydreams, only slightly less so. She has to admit that often in school only half her mind is present, the other half drifting into a second world where completely unlikely things occur. Love! Lust! Passion! And more. Oh, the headlines! GRACE BIHALLY SCORES AGAIN ON BROADWAY. . . . GRACE, YEAR'S MOST SOUGHT-AFTER ACTRESS . . . WILL SHE WIN ANOTHER OSCAR? . . . She adores the theater. She's in Drama Club, and her mother buys season tickets for the two of them for the Open Palm Repertory Theater every year.

But most of all, she loves her daydreams. In them, she strides freely, she's a star, playing roles that are dramatic and fabulous and hers because the director wanted someone big enough to handle them. Someone with a big presence, and a big self, and a big voice that moves freely into the world. A voice that's heard, not hushed.

NORMA FOX MAZER

She's not alone in these theaters of the mind. Her dreams are inhabited by men, by boys, by *males* — or, to put it another way, ever present is that human creature with the usual quota of arms, legs, eyes, et cetera, plus a flat chest and a penis. Hmmm . . . that last item — why does that one organ mean so much? Why does she imagine it so often? Why, walking the halls, do her eyes wander downward? Why does she even see it in her dreams?

For that matter, why must she always dream of men and boys? She's cool. She's accepting. She wouldn't, on principle, object to a dream now and then about a girl, a woman, a female. But no, in and out of sleep, day or night, winter or summer, it's males. And not always the ones she'd choose.

Mr. Vronsky is not an anomaly. Her dreams are often rich in other totally unsuitable and unwanted types. She once dreamed about a politician as well known for his florid, handsome face as his Maine accent and tight-lipped opinions about those people who "don't pull their own weight in society": unmarried girls with babies, whom he has scolded publicly and at length for not "controlling" their "wayward sexual urges." As if he, pure soul, had never had a wayward urge of any kind in his life!

In the dream about him, she was sitting on a stool and he, in a chair, was tenderly stroking her leg, while at the same time talking to someone else. *Men make*

GOING FISHING

the best monsters. Those were his dream words. *Yes, the best,* Grace had cried, her voice rising to a crescendo, and she thought how brilliant he was, and all the time he was stroking her leg, but as if he didn't know what he was doing, and she was staring up into his face, breathless and quivering.

Now that she's remembering all of her disgusting dreams, how about the one with Mr. Naples? Oh, she is perverted! Mr. Naples of the thinning hair and bad breath? Mr. Naples, her father's friend? A man she has never, ever, had the least, tiniest thought about as an object of desire? He and her father talk about the stock market, the stock market, the stock market. They are the definition of dull.

In the dream, though, Mr. Naples's effect on her was far from dull. He smiled into her eyes and said, *Grace.* Only that, only her name, and it drove her completely crazy. For at least a week, she went around with the dazed thought of him in her mind.

Fortunately for her sanity, he came over to visit with her father again. "Hello, Grace," he said.

"Hello . . . Mr. Naples." She had stared at him in amazement. There he was in all his boring glory. She had dreamed about *him*? Why?

No answer.

No answer, either, to why Vronsky this time, or why she has never dreamed about the one person she would welcome into every dream. A. B. Lovely A. B.

Does he elude her dreams because she won't allow herself to even think his name? Will permit only his initials into her mind? Silly initials, as if made up in some kindergarten of love. Anyway, it is all hopeless. She can never have him. She is twice as big, three times as clumsy, nowhere near as athletic. He is beautiful, graceful, popular. Everything she isn't. And he is her secret, her hopeless secret. One more hopeless thing about her.

She sits up, swings bare broad feet onto the floor. Faith is still curled up in the next bed, mouth half open, silver nails clutching the sheet protectively near her neck. Grace glances at her younger sister with the old, odd, and familiar mixture of anger and tenderness, then strips off the Redskins shirt she sleeps in. *Do not look in the mirror.* It's an order to herself, but one she disobeys. She can rarely resist the reality of herself, the need to force acceptance. *This is me. This is what God or genes or Mom and Dad gave me.*

The look is quick. She doesn't need a long look.

In a flash, she sees the massive body, sees how she defies and distorts and disturbs the image of a "normal" girl, of what a girl is "supposed" to be. The height of her, the width of her, the bones of her, the large breasts, the rounded stomach, the heavy thighs. Girl? Nothing girlish or feminine here. (It's at this moment she always remembers that day in the cafeteria hearing someone call her a buffalo.)

In grade school, when she was already larger than anybody, the teacher had read the class a book called *Stuart Little*, about a child born as small as a mouse. Grace, as large as Stuart was small, had felt a deep kinship with him, imagining that her parents must have felt exactly like this when she was born — dismayed and startled. Normal-sized people giving birth, in Stuart's case, to a mouse-sized child. In her case, to a whale-sized child. She had weighed over thirteen pounds at birth. Nothing could have prepared her poor parents for that. Both her older brothers had been a normal six pounds, and so was Faith when she was born a few years later. In the midst of all this normalcy — Grace.

She had written a story about Stuart Little that year. He was in his car, off to see what he could see. Along the way, he caused excitement everywhere. People turned out in droves to admire him. The best part of the story, though, was when he met Grace. Alone in her room, she would act out this scene.

"You're Miss Grace Bihally?" she would cry in a tiny Stuart Little voice, from a crouched position. "You can't imagine how delighted I am to meet you." Springing to her full height, she would look at the floor and return the greeting. "Mr. Stuart Little! *You* can't imagine how I admire you!" And then off they'd go to have adventures together.

At some point, it came to her that while small is

cute, even adorable, large is simply awkward and unpleasant. She began to wonder if, unlike Stuart Little, who was born to his family, she had slipped into hers by some horrid mistake. In the supermarket with her mother, she would stand by the checkout counter, reading the stories of lost children and mistaken identity in the newspapers lining the racks. PARENTS DISCOVER ONLY CHILD NOT THEIRS, ACTUALLY BELONGS TO FAMILY OF TEN. . . . KIDNAPPED BOY FINDS DYING FATHER AFTER FIVE-YEAR SEARCH. . . . NURSES ADMIT MISTAKE, BABIES SWITCHED AT BIRTH.

She had gulped down these stories, diving right into them, right into a big wet pool of poor-me-in-the-wrong-family fantasies, heart pushing in her chest until she got to the happy ending. Because, of course, the child in the wrong family was always an unhappy child, sometimes a badly treated child, ordered around, not fed well, made to do all the hardest tasks. Only when reunited with her true family would the lost child, at last, find the happiness she deserved. *Sniffle. Sniffle.*

Grace got older. She left behind both Stuart Little and lost-child fantasies. Luckily. Tears don't become her. Something else she knew about herself.

Faith mutters something in her sleep. Pretty Faith. Small Faith, perfectly formed Faith, graceful, feminine Faith. Faith, who could never be mistaken for the child of any other family.

"Oh, *hell*," Grace says. It comes over her like that sometimes.

"Whaat?" Faith mumbles anxiously in her sleep, disturbed by Grace's voice.

Like everything about her, it's large, outsized. It's nearly another presence, her voice. "Sleep, Faithy. It's okay."

She bends to tie her sneakers, remembering how, once, in her Stuart Little phase, she had bargained with herself that if she could stand on her left foot for an hour, Stuart would appear. She couldn't, and he didn't.

She stands now, bends her right leg back, and holds her foot against her butt. Nothing to it. She stands like that for a minute, two minutes, five minutes. Heck, she could do this for an hour. Maybe Stuart would show up this time.

The birds are starting to sing. She'd better get going. She picks up her faded, gray fedora, a hat that her entire family unites in disliking. They think it makes her look like a bag lady. She puts it on. She doesn't just like this hat, she loves it. She found it in a Salvation Army bin and embellished it with buttons that her mother wore back in the days before she became who she is now. The buttons say corny things like *Question authority. . . . Delight in disagreeing. . . . Women hold up half the sky*. It's amazing to think that her mother once wore these opinions boldly on sweaters and jackets. "My rebellious phase," her mother says, blinking, as if that time were a door to nothing that she had passed through.

Grace goes down the hall. Her mother comes out of her bedroom, tying her blue robe. "Hello, sweetie," she whispers, and before Grace can answer, her finger flies to her lips. They go down the stairs together.

"You're going fishing now?" her mother says, as if hoping she's got it wrong. As if, after all these years, she's still stunned by this large daughter, so different, so unlike herself. Not that she has ever said such a thing. She wouldn't, and nobody in the family would. Grace is treated (no other word for it) wonderfully. Her parents defer to her, respect her, love her. Her sister and brothers — well, they're sibs. They're fine. They accept her as she is. They all do. They try to, anyway. They try their best.

Grace hears herself thinking these things. *They try to . . . they try their best.* And knows that she's always known this, that it's the truth: they *try*, her family. They do try. But why must they *try*? Why can't they just do it?

This answer, she knows. Because who she is, is strange to them. She has always, in some fashion, known this, too.

And now she thinks that maybe the dreams she lives in, the daydreams and the night dreams, are there to help her make her way through her life, to help her stand steady, even when her big legs want to crumple.

But just now, on her way fishing, standing under her mother's anxious gaze, Grace has another dream, maybe a vision, in which she sees herself walking down a road into a spreading, diffuse white light, a light that leads her on, as if it's a silken rope she's holding, leads her on and on, and away and away . . .

"What?" her mother says.

She must have made a noise.

Grace shakes her head. "Nothing, Mom. I'll be home around ten," she says, consciously subduing her voice.

"I'll have breakfast for you." Her mother pats Grace's arm, a soothing familiar gesture.

Grace has always loved her mother's touch, but now she has the surprising notion that her mother is afraid of her and touches her this way to keep her soothed and smoothed, undangerous, as if there's some strange mechanism inside her (the one that has made her so unlike all her mother's other children), which might, if not handled gingerly, explode.

Grace walks to the door, trying not to rock the floor, trying, for her mother's sake, to seem smaller, quieter, *less*.

Today, she thinks, she'll come back. But one day she'll walk out the door and keep walking, just keep walking until she finds — well, what? The light? A place where she belongs? A place in the world where she can be as big and strong and loud — as *Grace* — as she was born, as she naturally is? Is there such a place? Is it possible?

Yes. She hears that. It comes from neither inside her nor outside her. It simply is. *Yes.* And for a moment, right there in the ordinary doorway of her ordinary home, she stands in the white light and seems to understand everything, the chief thing being *yes.* Yes, there is such a place. It's an instant of grace. Grace's grace. It's an instant only, and then it's gone, and she's out the door, and the morning light draws her on, big-footed, big-voiced, big-herself Grace.

The Transformations of Cindy R.

"Cin, Cin, *Cindy!*" the three girls call out. "Cindy! Will you help me put up the decorations for the dance?" Agnes says.

"Could you find my scissors, Cindy?" Marybeth chimes in.

"We need more cups!" Dara cries. "Cindy, where are the cups?"

Cindy hurries over. "Here I come, Agnes," she says in a low voice. "Okay, Marybeth. I'll find them, Dara."

Agnes is small and exquisite. Marybeth is strong and graceful. Dara is tall, dark, and statuesque. All three girls are beautiful. And popular. And busy.

Cindy is only busy. She sweeps the floor, brushes off the costumes, puts up the posters, runs the errands, counts the money, twists the crepe paper into bright spirals and hangs it from the gymnasium ceiling.

"You're serving the punch tonight, aren't you, Cindy?" Agnes says. It isn't really a question.

Cindy nods. Of course she is. She always serves the punch. She never dances.

If you look at her eyes — you don't, nobody does — but if you did, you'd wonder why blue eyes are considered attractive. Cindy's eyes do not remind anyone of the sky or the sea. Faded blue jeans have more color. Worn flannel sheets possess more sparkle. Old dishwater is more lively.

As for her hair, it hangs there, lank and mousy and dull, without even the energy to snarl. Her nose is nondescript, her mouth twists nervously whenever anyone asks her a question. Her eyes blink. She bites her lips, she whispers, she winds her hair around her fingers and then chews on it.

"Where'd you get the shirt, Cin?" Agnes takes the sleeve between her thumb and forefinger. It's a flannel shirt, big and baggy, like Cindy's other clothes.

"My brother," Cindy says.

"Give it back to your brother," Agnes says. "The color's all wrong. You look washed out."

"Oh," says Cindy. She imagines her face like a piece of cloth, loose and empty. Her shoulders slump even more.

Agnes turns away. A tall boy has just walked into

the gymnasium. He has broad shoulders and shaggy blond hair. His eyes are blue and sparkling.

"Jeff!" Dara cries, holding open her arms.

Marybeth runs to him, but it is Agnes who gets there first. She puts her hand on his arm and smiles triumphantly at the other two.

"Let's go for ice cream," Jeff says. "Are we done working?"

"Cindy will finish," says Dara. "Won't you, Cindy?"

Cindy glances at the posters on the floor, the unfurled wheels of crepe paper, the piles of dust in the corners of the gymnasium, and nods. "Of course," she says. She always does.

Jeff links arms with Agnes and Marybeth, while Dara follows somewhat sulkily behind.

No one asks Cindy to go for ice cream. She wouldn't dream of it, anyway. Broom in hand, she hurries around the gymnasium, making sure everything is ready for the dance.

Tonight Cindy will stand behind the refreshment table, pouring punch and serving cookies on paper plates. Dara, Agnes, and Marybeth will all dance with Jeff, who will gaze adoringly at each in turn. Dara will be splendid in a rose gown that sets off her dark hair and eyes. Agnes will be exquisite in white with a wreath of flowers in her pale hair. Marybeth will wear a braided ribbon around her neck and a dress of many colors, and as she dances, she will look like a fountain shooting off sparks of colored light.

Cindy will wear a dress that Marybeth gave her. It is dark blue and tight in the shoulders, too short, and the zipper cuts into her back. On Marybeth it looked graceful and lovely, but it's cut all wrong for Cindy. But it's better at least than her only other dress, a shapeless brown tent also handed down to her.

When Cindy pours the punch tonight, she will try not to spill it on her classmates. Otherwise Agnes might yell — she has a temper. When the dance is done, Cindy will sweep up, count the money, and put it in a safe. Then she will go home, eke out a few tears, and fall asleep.

But it doesn't happen like that.

At seven o'clock, Cindy goes home to eat and change into her dress. Her mother has left her supper on the plate. The mashed potatoes are cold and lumpy, and a thin layer of grease has congealed over the roast beef.

"What do you expect when you come home at all hours?" her mother complains. "I'm not a servant, you know."

"Sorry," Cindy says.

"Sorry isn't enough. You ought to help out a little more. I'm tired. I've been working all day. Don't expect to get out of here tonight without doing the dishes and mopping the floor."

ANNE MAZER

68 STAY TRUE

To drown out the sound of her mother's nagging, Cindy picks up a magazine. As she turns the pages, her eye is caught by a picture of one of those ceramic statues that you buy in six installments of $24.99 a month.

"Yes, you, too, can own this enchanting one-of-a-kind figurine," says the ad. "Your very own fairy godmother will watch over and protect you with her realistic magic wand. Hand-painted silver stars decorate the edges of her robe. Tiny crystal slippers adorn her feet. Produced in a very limited edition by the acclaimed European porcelain artist, Tiddly Wink."

"And *blah, blah, blah,*" Cindy says. But she takes another quick look at the fairy godmother. And then she grabs a pen and begins filling out the order form. It's silly, really; she doesn't know why she's doing it. For one thing she doesn't have the money; for another, she doesn't like painted porcelain statues. But something is pushing her — almost like a hand on her back, a voice in her ear — that she can't resist.

Cindy fills in her name, address, phone number, and age, then carefully tears out the coupon. If anyone needs a fairy godmother, it's her, even if it's a phony porcelain one.

And she puts the coupon in her pocket, thinking that maybe she'll mail it later.

But it doesn't happen that way.

Poof! A small figure has appeared on the table in

front of her, right between the dinner plate and the water glass. She is about six inches tall, with pretty porcelain cheeks, and bright blue eyes. She is wearing a long, flowing silk gown with hand-painted stars along the hem and sleeves.

"Oh!" Cindy cries out, then claps her hand over her mouth.

The figurine is beautifully made. She almost seems to breathe. Slowly Cindy reaches out and touches the masses of silver hair piled into a bun.

"Stop poking at me!" snaps the figurine.

Cindy hastily withdraws her hand.

"I'm your fairy godmother," she says with a haughty toss of her head. "In case you didn't notice."

Cindy feels in her pocket for the coupon, but it's gone. And she didn't even mail it.

The fairy godmother casts a shrewd, appraising glance at her and whistles low under her breath. "You're a mess," she says. "No wonder you called me."

"I actually never called you." Cindy twists a strand of lank hair around her finger and starts to chew on it. "I mean, I meant to . . ."

"Oh, stop blathering!" says the fairy godmother. "Take it from me. I can fix you up good. I know just what you need."

"You do?" Cindy asks.

"Cindy! Did you clear the dishes? Is the floor

washed? Don't forget to take out the garbage!" her mother calls from the other room.

"You need me." The fairy godmother raises a tiny golden wand. "Put yourself under my tutelage. All you have to say is yes and you'll be completely transformed. Is that an offer you can refuse?"

Cindy opens her mouth, then shuts it. Does she really want a fairy godmother that much? Have things gotten to that point? Hasn't she been getting along fine? Well, maybe not *fine*, but she's coping.

"Do you hear me, Cindy?" her mother says. "Answer me! If that kitchen isn't completely clean when I come in, you can forget about the dance!"

"Okay," Cindy says to the fairy godmother.

"Okay, what?" the fairy godmother retorts. "Follow instructions! You have to say yes."

"Yes!" Cindy says.

The fairy godmother waves her wand. *Poof!* The dishes are washed, the floor is clean, the garbage is empty.

"Cindy!!" her mother calls.

"All done, Mom!" She picks up the fairy godmother and runs up the stairs to her room.

"Stand over there." The fairy godmother points to the corner. "Take off those clothes," she orders.

"Do I have to?" Cindy shrinks back. But at the commanding look in the fairy godmother's eye, she takes off first the big faded flannel shirt her brother gave her, then the baggy jeans, the sneakers and heavy socks, and finally the old T-shirt she wears over her underwear.

Cindy wraps her arms around herself. Her skin is too pale, her arms and legs too long, her hips are too narrow, and her breasts too small. It doesn't help that she needed to buy new underwear six months ago. Three safety pins hold her bra together; her underpants are ripped at the seams.

The fairy godmother gives her a sharp, appraising glance. "You don't have a bad figure, you know. You should show it off more."

"Uh . . ." Cindy doesn't know what to say. She wishes that she could melt into the floor. The fairy godmother mutters a few words to herself, then waves her wand again. The air rustles like silk and releases the scent of a hundred flowers. *Poof!* A large mirror appears across from Cindy. She stares at the stranger reflected there. Who is it? She doesn't recognize herself. She is completely transformed.

Her hair is piled on her head in shining, graceful curls. The blush on her cheeks and lips is not natural, but it has been so artfully applied that no one can tell.

And then there is the dress. It is pale apricot, with a long sweeping skirt, a tightly cut bodice, and lace-covered sleeves. Her feet are shod in matching apricot-colored slippers. There are rings on her fingers and a velvet choker around her neck.

"You're a vision," says the fairy godmother, clasping her hands.

Cindy twirls around. The dress is looped in the back, with a full sash. Indeed, the dress is so full of lace and ribbons and bows, hoops and sleeves and sashes, that she feels as if she could set sail in it.

She frowns at herself in the mirror, wondering if she has new underwear, too, perhaps something in French silk. To tell the truth, she's not that crazy about the dress.

"What's the matter?" the fairy godmother demands. "Don't you like it?"

"It's the color," Cindy says hesitantly. If she asks for a simpler dress, she might offend the fairy godmother. "Don't you think blue or violet would look better on me?"

The fairy godmother shakes her head. "You young girls just don't know left from right, or up from down. The color is perfect for you, trust me."

Cindy nods. "Okay." It's what she's been saying all her life to everyone.

"This dress will change your life," the fairy godmother says. "It will make you happy. And beautiful. And loved."

Cindy looks at herself again. She resembles an overdressed box of candy. She's never seen Agnes, or

Dara, or Marybeth wearing anything like this. "Really? You're sure?"

The fairy godmother has a tinkling, chimelike laugh. "You'll be the belle of the ball. Do you know how to dance?"

"No." Her voice quavers a little. Even when she gets a break from serving punch, she always stands at the edge of the crowd and watches the others dance. No one has ever asked her to dance. Not even the other girls want to dance with her.

The fairy godmother raises the tiny golden wand again and points it at Cindy's feet. *Poof!* They begin to tingle. Heat rushes to her toes. She begins to move. One, two, three; one, two, three. Step, glide, step. Cindy swirls and swoops around her bedroom as if she's done it for a lifetime, while the fairy godmother claps in time.

"Bravo!" the fairy godmother cries. "Bravo! Babe, you're terrific!"

Cindy comes to a halt. Was that really her, Cindy, dancing? Automatically she reaches up for a strand of hair to chew on.

"Oh, no! None of that!" The fairy godmother waves her wand once more. *Poof!*

Cindy's hand freezes in midair. How could she ever have chewed on her hair? What a disgusting habit! The very thought of it makes her stomach churn.

ANNE MAZER

As she lowers her hand, Cindy notices that her nails are all perfectly shaped and polished a pale apricot. She wants to bite them, but somehow she can't. She can only gaze admiringly at the sapphire-and-gold rings on her fingers.

She dances a few steps, then halts in front of the mirror. Is that really her, she wonders again. She's like a little girl dressed up in her mother's clothes. Everyone is going to see through this costume.

"Oh!! Oh!!!" Cindy cries out at the very thought of it. Tears streak down her face, but her makeup does not smear.

She knows what is going to happen. They are going to send her to the washroom to scrub off the makeup and change back into her old, dark hand-me-downs. Then she will return to serve punch all night to Jeff and Marybeth and Dara and Agnes, and everything will be the way it's always been.

But it doesn't happen like that.

When Cindy walks into the room, everyone falls silent and stares at her. She panics, she wants to run, but in these shoes, she'd fall on her face.

But no, instead, a girl named Alicia, who has never spoken to Cindy before, cries, "You look so *fabulous!*"

The fairy godmother is right. The dress is a hit; it

transforms the evening. Everyone loves it. Everyone loves her.

"That dress!" Dara moans.

"Who does your hair?" Marybeth cries.

"Those bows!" Agnes screams. "And the lace, too!"

"You're stunning! Beautiful! Fabulous!" The compliments rain down on her like flowers.

Do they recognize her? No one calls her by name. They all stare at her with big eyes. Can they be envious eyes?

As Cindy walks — or rather glides — across the gymnasium, Jeff takes her hand and says, "Will you dance?"

Cindy nods. This really is a fairy tale. The music begins. They dance together as if they've done it all their lives. She moves as if enchanted — and of course she is. She only hopes there are no side effects; after all, she never takes so much as an aspirin.

Jeff gazes adoringly into her eyes. "You're beautiful," he says. "That color . . . what is it?"

"Apricot," Cindy says.

His fingers brush against the fabric. "So delicious, so lovely, so soft . . ."

She feels like a piece of fruit ready to be gobbled. "It's not edible."

As they dance around and around, not missing a

step, his eyes never leave her face. "I *know* I've seen you before."

"Yes," Cindy says. "You've seen me before."

"Where?"

Cindy almost smiles. "Maybe in another life."

"I knew it!" he cries out triumphantly.

He leans toward her and whispers in her ear, "We were meant to be together."

Cindy is beginning to have her doubts. Did he actually say those words? "Meant to be together?" How corny can you get? Dancing with Jeff isn't all it's cracked up to be. This conversation is actually dumber than dumb, and she's beginning to feel a little annoyed by all the other girls staring and smiling at her.

She glances over at the refreshment table. A thin, dark girl in an ill-fitting dress is pouring drinks. Cindy doesn't wish she were back there again, but she doesn't one hundred percent like where she is, either. Maybe not even ninety percent. Or even eighty.

The music stops. She sighs with relief, but Jeff won't let her go.

"I want the next dance and the next dance and the next," he says.

But her feet hurt. She wonders if the fairy godmother goofed and made the slippers too tight. Could a fairy godmother make a mistake? "I want to sit down."

"You can't." Jeff holds her arm tightly. "I'll die of unhappiness if I can't have just one more dance. Please."

Now he's definitely getting on her nerves. Maybe it's that pleading but possessive look in his eyes, or maybe it's that he's not listening to anything she says.

Cindy tries to pull away, but he won't let her go.

"Dance with me now," he insists.

Tears well up in her eyes. "Please . . ." she mutters.

Then she stops and takes a breath. She is different tonight. She's not the old shy, scared Cindy. The fairy godmother has transformed her, made her a new person. Very well, she will be that new person.

She smiles sweetly at Jeff, and then kicks him hard in the shins.

In the bathroom, where she has escaped, dozens of girls mob her. They want to know about the dress, about her hair, her makeup, how she made Jeff fall in love with her so quickly, and why he looked so forlorn and stunned just now on the dance floor.

"What's your secret?" Agnes asks breathlessly.

"I have a fairy godmother," Cindy says, pretending to touch up her makeup. It still looks as flawless as when she left the house.

The other girls laugh.

"What's it like dancing with Jeff?" asks a shy, plump girl.

"Boring."

"Is anyone else going to get to dance with Jeff tonight?" This is Dara speaking.

"I hope so," Cindy says.

"How come we've never seen you before?" one of the girls demands.

Cindy shrugs. "But you have. I always served the punch at the refreshment table."

"No — not you! Cindy's the one who always does it. Have you ever run into her? She's nothing like you. You'd never allow yourself to even be seen with her!" Dara, Marybeth, Agnes, and the other girls laugh.

They don't know who she is. They think she's beautiful and poised and glamorous. They smooth her dress, tug at her bows, pat the ribbons in her hair.

"We want to see how this lace is made. How did you get your hair to curl on top of your head like that? Are your shoes made of silk?"

Touching, prodding, and admiring, they crowd her into a corner. Cindy can barely breathe. "Give me some air, girls," she pleads.

They don't listen to her.

Once again, she is about to burst into tears. But again she stops. This is her night; she is the belle of the ball. She is not shy, scared, slouching, slumping

Cindy anymore. She's a new person. She already had a trial run with Jeff. She just needs some more practice.

Cindy opens her mouth and yells at the top of her lungs, "BUG OFF!"

Dara, Marybeth, Agnes, and the others flee.

Cindy smiles at herself in the bathroom mirror. She rips away her sash, kicks off the uncomfortable slippers, ties them to a loop on her dress, and walks barefoot to the gymnasium.

Jeff is waiting for her. He is limping slightly, but his eyes still light up when he sees her. "The next dance?" he asks, eyeing her bare feet and the slippers dangling from her dress.

"No, thank you."

"We have to see each other again. You're so — different." He reaches for her hand, but she jerks it away and runs off.

She looks back once at Jeff. Good riddance! she thinks. That's the end of that.

It is ten minutes before midnight. Cindy is looking forward to getting off this horrid dress, scrubbing all the makeup from her face, and having a long, hot soak in the tub.

But it doesn't happen like that.

Her parents are asleep when Cindy lets herself in with the key, but the fairy godmother is awake. Her blue porcelain eyes glitter with excitement as she paces back and forth on the shelf next to Cindy's bed.

"Well? How was it?"

"Different," Cindy says.

"The experience of a lifetime?"

"Yes."

"I knew it would be!" the fairy godmother crows triumphantly.

"I hated it."

The fairy godmother crosses her arms. "And just what was so bad about it, Miss Unreasonable? Weren't you the most beautiful girl at the dance? The belle of the ball? Didn't the most handsome boy fall in love with you?"

"Yes, yes, yes . . ." With clumsy fingers, Cindy unfastens the dress. "Can you help me get these hoops off?"

The fairy godmother points the wand at Cindy's costume. *Poof!* It's gone. All that's left is a sash and a pair of slippers. She's sitting in her underwear again. At least it's French silk.

"You had an evening any girl would die for," says the fairy godmother, stamping her tiny porcelain foot. "How can you complain?"

Cindy tosses the apricot slippers to the floor. "You made them too tight," she says. "I could hardly breathe in that dress. And Jeff is a bore."

"Picky, picky, picky. Don't let little details stand in the way of your happiness."

"You call this happiness?" Cindy tugs at the pins in her hair.

"It will be soon. We haven't even begun . . ." The fairy godmother has a determined look that Cindy doesn't like. "By next week, every boy in the school will be mad for you."

"No, thank you," says Cindy, imagining a long line of Jeffs approaching her with that stubborn, possessive gleam in their eyes.

"We'll wow 'em," says the fairy godmother. "We'll pow 'em. They'll love you. They won't leave you alone."

"*No*, thank you!"

"Tonight was just a warm-up." The fairy godmother's eyes sparkle. "Wait until you see what I can really do." She waves her wand again and again.

Poof! Poof! Poof! As if in a slide show, Cindy sees herself in one outfit after another. There are leggings in bright colors, cabled sweaters, gauzy blouses with lace and pearl buttons, silk skirts that cling, jungle print dresses, leather boots, and matching backpacks. . . . And her hair is short, long, wavy, straight, piled on her head, cascading around her shoulders, curling over her ears.

It makes her dizzy to see herself in so many ways. She can hardly remember what she really looks like.

"Enough!" she cries. "Please! I don't want to see anymore."

The fairy godmother's eyes burn more brightly than ever. She points her wand at Cindy again.

"We'll redo your face," she says. "Make your nose a little straighter and your eyes a little larger. We'll put highlights in your hair, sculpt your thighs, and add an extra inch to your bra size. We'll change your name to Cinda. No, to Synda, Cyndina . . ."

"Stop!" Cindy cries.

The fairy godmother keeps waving her wand. Cindy, Cinda, Synda, Cyndina, or whoever she is now, seizes the fairy godmother, plucks the wand from her fingers, and breaks it in two.

Instantly Cindy — no doubt who she is now — returns to her former self. The straight, lank brown hair. The flat chest. The ripped underwear held together by pins.

"You'll be sorry!" sobs the fairy godmother, her little porcelain features distorted by rage. "A fairy godmother's curse on you! You'll go back to serving sodas! You're nothing without me! Twerp! Hussy! Brat! Ingrate!"

Knowing that in fairy tales, it's always important to be polite, Cindy smiles and says, "Thank you," once more before she picks up the shrieking figurine and drops her onto the bare floor, where she shatters into a thousand pieces.

Cindy sweeps her up carefully. She wouldn't want to cut herself on pieces of her fairy godmother.

At school the next day, between classes, she runs into Dara, Agnes, and Marybeth.

"Where were you last night?" Agnes complains. "We had to find someone else to serve the punch. And no one swept the floor."

"You've got to start making posters for the next dance," says Dara.

"And I have a dress for you to mend," Marybeth adds. "I need it by tomorrow."

"Tomorrow?" Cindy's eyes prickle with tears. "I can't possibly —" Suddenly she stops. Is she still shy, scared, slumping, slouching Cindy? Is she still going to sweep the floor, mend the dress, make the posters? Now that she isn't the new Cindy anymore, is she the old Cindy again?

It might happen that way . . . or maybe it won't.

Cindy faces the three girls.

"I'm out of the picture," she says. Her voice begins to quaver, but she takes a breath and goes on. "Mend your own dress, Marybeth."

"What?" The girls stare at her in shock.

Cindy stands up straighter. "Make your own posters," she says.

Her mouth is firm. Her eyes are clear. Her voice is

strong. This isn't a fairy tale anymore, so when she smiles, she isn't being polite.

She walks away. And then turns and yells, "Sweep your own floors!"

And that's the end of that.

She made it happen that way.

Crazy as a Daisy

Any other day of the week Daddy was the beast we ran from the minute the Buick pulled into the driveway. We'd hide and wait for him to be fed and put to bed before we sat at the table to eat food we knew he was not served. His plate — I've seen it — was an overflow of rice, beans, and cornbread around meat with a bone. My sister, Rosalyn, and I ate either Chef Boyardee ravioli, fish sticks, or burned TV dinners, and loved them.

This Friday evening would be different.

Rosalyn and I sat on the velvet sofa in our crinoline sundresses, waiting for Daddy to walk through the door. I couldn't keep still, banging my ashy legs against the sofa, anticipating something spectacular. Dreamy even. All week long Daddy had promised us dance lessons, and tonight was the night.

Daddy never did anything common, because, in his own words, the streets were littered with common Jacks and Joneses. So, before we could have lessons, we had lectures on how to sit, cross our legs, and fold our hands. "Just remember one thing," Daddy said. "A lady's eyes never beg a dance. A lady waits to be asked."

We heard the car pulling in. All my boyfriend thoughts jumped to life when Daddy walked through the door wearing his Class A army uniform. These were thoughts reserved in my five-year-old heart for Chiefie (this half-colored, half-Japanese boy in my kindergarten class), Prince Charming from the nickel matinee, and Sam Cooke from Mama's record cover. On Sunday drives with the car windows rolled tight, I'd use the smoke from Mama's and Daddy's Salems to transport myself to the Cinderella Ballroom where boyfriend thoughts danced all out. While Elvis worked his most colored-sounding voice on the radio, I'd paste my face onto Cinderella, and Chiefie's face onto Prince Charming, and the cigarette smoke would send us gliding from one star to the next.

Just as we had hoped, Daddy didn't forget about the lessons. Instead of changing into his civvies, he went straight to the record cabinet and selected his favorite, The Platters. It was one of my favorites, too. I imagined Mama, before she got married, looked

RITA WILLIAMS-GARCIA

like the golden-haired, pecan-skinned woman on the cover.

Daddy blew the dust off the record player needle and laid the arm down gently on the spinning vinyl. I giggled as he gave one final demonstration of the curtsy before the actual dance lesson. Not because his movements were uncharacteristically feminine, but because I had been practicing my wobble-free curtsy all afternoon, and was anxious to show it off.

Awaiting my turn, I was the most perfect lady I could be, with my legs stuck together, my spine erect, and my hands folded in my lap to hide my nails, blackened from dirt clod fighting.

Daddy bowed, extended his arm to my seven-year-old sister, and said, "Mademoiselle, may I have the pleasure of this dance?"

At that moment Mama stepped out with a casserole dish in her mitted hands, rolled her eyes, and did the cha-cha back into the kitchen.

"Sure, Daddy."

Hmph! I who knew of Brigitte Bardot, Leslie Caron, and Pepe Le Pew would have said, *"Wee wee, meshuur."* I felt pins of envy prick me as I watched my sister follow Daddy's lead.

Daddy was a good dancer. This came from his days as a bebop boy singing on the corner with The Young War Lords. Thanks to Mama, I knew Papa was once a slouching teenager who wolf whistled at girls. Not even my sister was privy to this treasured secret.

Finally, "My Prayer" faded. I banged my legs against the sofa, unable to contain myself. Their hands unjoined. Daddy bowed and said, "*Merci beaucoup, Mademoiselle.*" My sister curtsied the way he had shown us and sat back down, careful to cross her legs.

It was my turn. Excited, I jumped the gun, extending my hand instead of waiting for the invitation. To my complete disappointment Daddy stretched, expelling a lion's yawn before deflating, taking Chiefie, Prince Charming, and Sam Cooke with him.

"I want dance lessons, too, Daddy."

Daddy loosened his Class A army tie and said, "Marguerite, nobody gonna ask you to dance." And that was that.

I was grateful Rosalyn never brought up my being left hanging on the dance floor. I prepared myself for relentless torture like the time she looked up her name in the dictionary and sang "Beautiful as a Rose" day and night until Mama popped her one. I looked up my name hoping it would say "stargazer" or "dirt clod conqueror" or "really smart for five years old." Instead it said, "Crazy as a daisy." I was stunned but wouldn't show it. Instead, I boasted as loud as I could, "Marguerite! Crazy as a daisy. That's right!"

and pranced around in crazy daisy fashion casting my arms, legs, and barrettes to the wind.

After that I danced all the time. On the outside I wore a towel for a wig and white go-go boots; on the inside I was the short Ikette à la Ike and Tina Turner. I'd watch the white kids on *American Bandstand*, the black kids on *Soul Train*, and the champagne dancers on *The Lawrence Welk Show*, and outdance them all.

I was invited to my first house party at the age of ten. Actually it was Veroy's birthday party. His voice was deep and raspy for twelve and his head reminded me of Secret Squirrel's, but I didn't care. The forty-fives were spinning, which kept me dancing all night long, and I knew Veroy liked me.

The girls danced genteel girl dances like the tip, a girl version of the funky four corners, and the philly-dog, on one side of the room. The boys did warrior dances — the James Brown and the camel walk — in the middle of the rug. Then out of a blare of horns, JB screamed, "I gat the feelin-uh," and the soles of my shoes got slippery. I was on the center of the rug doing the JB with the boys, fixing to do a split, when Rosalyn *yanked* me hard and pulled me over to the girls' side.

I didn't like girl-dancing. Girls danced like their daddies were watching, whereas boys jumped out like warriors cutting each other left and right with their

CRAZY AS A DAISY

mean turns and declarative arm movements that said, "Touch that if you dare!" I wanted to jump wild like a warrior, but with my own spin. Crazy as a daisy.

Just as I found myself inching away from the girls' side, the music changed. It got slower. Lower. I recognized it from my smoke-filled nights at the Cinderella Ballroom. Boy-leads-girl music. I sat down instinctively on the plastic-covered couch and in spite of myself, crossed my legs. After all the boys and girls paired, I waited for Veroy to ask me to dance. He looked my way but didn't make a move. Veroy and I popped wheelies and rode bikes together up Snake Hill. He hugged me when I scored the game-winning home run for our kickball team. Now my nails were clean. I had my hair pressed, I wore a dress, and I'd really brushed my teeth for a change. *He has to ask me to dance.* When it was apparent that no one, particularly Secret Squirrel-Headed Veroy, would, I got up and slow-dragged a crazy-as-a-daisy dance all by my lonesome. Rosalyn was mortified.

I continued to dance like a fool, throwing my arms to the wind. *Ya dance me, ya dance me not.* I could spin!

In junior high school, I joined a group — Anastasia and the Black Pearls. Anastasia would belt out Millie Jacksons and 'Retha Franklins, while me and two other girls "shoo-doo-wopped" and pantomimed her ninth-grade pain in the background.

RITA WILLIAMS-GARCIA

Then as a surprise to us all, Anastasia departed from her muddy ballads and decided to finish with a fast song to clinch our school's annual talent show. Suddenly . . . *Yeow! Good God-unh!* I got that slippery *dance me, dance me not* impulse all the way to my toes — *OW!* I couldn't stop myself, and I was out of the Black Pearls, not to mention laughed offstage.

Dancing in high school was another story altogether. I'd get nauseous at hooky parties with real boy-leads-girl dancing — knees finding their way between thighs, red lights, Mad Dog in the Hi-C punch. My warrior spirit completely surrendered. For the first time in my life, I actually cared what I looked like and if someone would extend his hand to save me from the wall. Once rescued, I'd stiffen in my savior's embrace, only to be quickly pushed away when the music died.

Fortunately everything changed in college. Liber-a-tion was the word. I celebrated it with earrings as big as birdcages, tie-dyed rags around my head, platform heels, peace-and-love gauze shirts, Peach Melba jeans, plenty protesting, petitioning, and every other Friday night dancing crazy as a daisy at Kappa and Alpha balls. All the frats and sororities printed flyers with NO SNEAKERS and DRESS TO IMPRESS, which meant: "Crazy Daisies go home." I'd get in somehow, find some gay boys who were all about bogarting the limelight, hang with them and dance just as crazy daisy as I wanted to. As the regular crowd did the hustle, and boys spun girls who gave ladylike attitude, I scattered myself to the wind, *dance me, dance me not*, and no one messed with me. Except one Friday night, some guy reached out and attempted to harness me into one of those hustle things. One-two, one-two-three. There was no escaping the GQ Robot with his jacket sleeves rolled up to his elbow and his hair dripping with curl juice, his grip unrelenting as he pushed me in and out, bending my hand to make me turn. I broke free the first chance I got and vowed never to dance like that, with anyone. Ever. After all, liberation was the word! I had to dance all out, throwing my daisies to the wind.

I really meant that, until I saw Roland. My heart went thud. Really. I saw him striding across the bridge that connected the learning side of the campus with the sleep-eating side, and there I was, a five-year-old gliding from star to star in the smoke-filled Cinderella Ballroom.

"He's a senior," another freshman cautioned me.

"He's gorgeous," was all I knew. I couldn't wait for him to notice me or ask me out — as neither were likely. So, I waited until he sat alone in the cafeteria, took my tray, and plunked myself down across from him. He was trapped.

"So, why haven't I seen you at any dances?"

"Because I won't dance," he said. And he looked annoyed. He was a thinker, and I was keeping him from himself. Who cared? I was staking out my claim on an astronomy major with his very own equation named after him. Something to do with the natural disintegration of stars. Rumor had it he started college at fourteen, which made him my age. Eighteen.

"I won't dance partnered," I offered.

"So I've heard." Was that a smirk?

"They talk about me?" I laughed. "I thought they just pointed."

"You're proud of that?"

"Why not? I'm uncommon and I love it."

"You're uncommon, all right."

"I'm not alone, Roland. I'll bet you've got all kinds of star-burning equations stored up there that no one's ever heard of."

Damn! He was fine.

"Are you making fun of me?"

"I'm just saying, you're uncommon. I'm uncommon. You should be my partner. Dance with me at the Q-Ball."

"I will not dance."

"With me?"

"Not with anyone."

Warrior undaunted. "Why not?"

"I will not dance."

CRAZY AS A DAISY

I was mesmerized. Did he know that everything he said had rhythm? And shapes? Rectangles. Triangles.

"But you *have* to dance with me." Why? Because you're mine, you uncommon fool! Instead I said, "I can show you."

We ate in silence, which I took for yes.

Truth be told, I loved to chase him even more than I loved staring at him, and he was gorgeous. At that moment I was face to face with my nature: Pursuing him made my warrior spirit dance all out. He'd paint himself inside a tight *no, I won't dance* box and I'd find an opening to spear him.

When I got him up to my dorm room, I couldn't tell if his trepidation was from the prospect of embarking on new ground or from the shock of being enclosed in the scattered mess that was my home. Before he could turn and run, I quickly pulled out my box of tapes and tossed cassettes about until I found it. "You'll like this," I said and slipped the tape in, then practically leaped before him. No. I *did* leap.

"You are my starship, come take me up tonight . . ."

"Listen to the music," I said, not knowing my voice could do that. The low, sensual thing. Zowie! I loved being female. "Count."

"Count?"

"Put your hands here," said my new voice.

He got all nervous and started to count. Real fast.

"Slow," I told him. "Um-hm. You count. I lead. That's it."

He followed me, at first feeling pretty foolish, but not about to let go. And when he trusted me and didn't have to count aloud or look at his feet, he surrendered to being led and asked, "Now what?"

To that, me and my all new voice replied, "Make like a daisy, and I'll spin ya."

The Pale Mare

"But why?" I ask again, even though I know what he'll say.

"Because it's tradition."

He always says that. My papa. He's not a tall man, but he has much height in the soaring ways of our family and *la raza*, too.

Papa leans against the shiny side of our vendor truck with the black script that announces *Diaz Family Food*. The heavy smell of grease and corn hangs over us like a banner, an invisible proclamation: tradition.

Our family as always is at the *charreada,* the Mexican-style rodeo, to sell tamales, burritos, refried beans, and sweet bread. The real stuff. Not the Taco Bell version.

I try a different angle. After all, I'm good in

geometry. "Papa, it's just this one, small weekend. Rafael can help."

My cousin. He helped last year when I had my appendix out. I wonder briefly if I have another body part to give out.

"Consuela," says Papa, then he bends over a sack of pinto beans. He lifts the fifty pounds as easy as my tiny baby sister and continues, "This is the final *charreada* and it is gonna be huge. I need your help. Not Rafael who goofs around."

I sigh. My expertise isn't what he needs. Any fool can take orders. It's not complicated to yell, "Four chicken burritos, one green sauce, three red, two large Cokes, two medium 7Ups." No, it's not my expertise in serving food that my precious parents want to preserve. It's that damn tradition again, our *familia* thing, the one that leads to *la raza*, the bigger picture of our people, who we are as Latin Americans. At least that's how Papa and Mama see it. But I don't see things just that way. Not anymore.

Papa goes into the house with the beans, for Mama to soak, then cook. I see my exit and in the dusk fling myself down the street, fast, furious, flying.

Kids play on the street, kicking soccer balls and riding bikes, rushing about like wasps from a knocked-down nest. As usual, it's the boys playing outside, with the rare girl running alongside until she can be gathered back into her house.

Papa is disgusted with my long walks. For once Mama tells him to let me be. She knows that I will explode like a star going nova if I am to stay home always.

Each of my strides jars a different, recent memory. Earlier this week at school: my teacher exclaiming over my work in physics, "Excellent work, Consuela. I'll write a letter of recommendation for you. You should really apply to Cal Tech and MIT. You're coming to the weekend astronomy camp, right?" My heart sang. The stars. For the last two years, they are all I've wanted to do: Study them, chart their fierce light, listen to them, learn what they are saying. Stars do talk — really — with radio waves for words. But when I got home from school, an eclipse was on.

Parents, on the dark side: "You will not go to any camp. Isn't school during the week enough? You have to help us with the business."

Me, trying to remain calm in the light: "What about, Manuel?" My brother, older by a year.

Parents, astonishment: "He has football practice."

"So what! I'm getting top honors in science! He's just playing junior varsity football!"

More genuine astonishment: "But he's the son." Meaning, of course, I'm only the daughter, only a girl. Maybe they don't mean to, but they're banishing me to the dark. I can't let that happen.

Later Mama tried to soothe me. "*M'ija,* it's because we love you. We want you to be happy with a nice boy, to have a family."

"Are you saying being an astronomer and being happy with a nice boy are not compatible?"

She *was* saying that with her hands that touched my hair, with her liquid Spanish murmuring, with her eyes that lingered on my face, imploring me to stop struggling in this foolish manner.

I cross busy Lincoln Avenue and head up Rio Hondo Road, past the earth dam. The oil hills, scrubby with ugly bushes, prickled with derricks, bunch up on one side, then unfurl into the familiar, sandy, flattened flood plain.

The night is clear, rare in smoggy L.A. My science class is at this moment zooming away from L.A. for a weekend at Joshua Tree. They will observe the breathtaking stars from the desert floor.

A sob shakes my lungs. I didn't even know I was crying, but tears drip down my chin and onto my shirt collar. Why didn't I just go, like my friend Mia suggested? Because I have these stupid ideals, like honesty.

I find that, as suddenly as I started, I've stopped crying. The wind, fresh and sharp, brings the hot scent of livestock, dirt, and human sweat.

The *charreada.*

The grounds are quiet. The arena is smooth as a

flour tortilla. Many of the *charros'* horses are stabled here in tidy, low barns, including the one belonging to *Tío* Jesús, Papa's brother. *Tío* Jesús' horse is an Andalusian, the color of very ripe plums.

The stock pens are on the far side, closest to the flood control, the citified riverbed that captures the water and hurries it to the sea, thirty miles away. Some of the water rushes from the San Gabriel Mountains, ten miles away, a dark stain in the north sky. The flood control is a hundred miles long, mountains to ocean. I've ridden this nearby stretch a million times, along its sandy path on my uncle's serious but kindly horse. Horses in the city — it sounds funny — the *charros,* they wouldn't have it any other way. Like my family. Life has to be a certain way. Their way.

Not for me though. Sorry, Papa, Mama. Your world isn't my world. It's not that I'm trying to pretend my Mexican blood doesn't course through my veins, it just means that my blood is calling to different things. That isn't wrong or bad.

Is it?

Mama, Papa, they just don't get it.

Or maybe they do. Perhaps that scares them.

I climb the sturdy metal pipe corral. I bypass the cattle, lumpy beasts dozing like logs in a stream, dull, empty of life, cut off from their roots, and head out to the edge of the corrals.

I've been going to *charreadas* since I was a baby. The smell of dirt and animals was often overlaid by the stronger scent of greasy bean burritos, but I'd always sniff and sniff until the odor of hot horses and freshly shaken alfalfa flakes overtook me. When I was really little I'd clap my hands and crow, *"Char, char."* I'd play I was a *charro* and swing astride the nearest fence, imagining I rode the finest horses — a Paso Fino, slate gray with white banners for a mane and tail, or a chestnut Andalusian, lifting his hooves high in the Spanish walk. The horse and I always moved as one — a seamless centaur.

What happened? Why did I change?

No moon tonight. My science class is observing stars tonight because a moonless night shows the stars the best. Starlight. I wish I could hold the light of those distant fires in my hands, bright and smooth as a sea stone, or maybe poured into a bowl and drunk like intoxicating tequila, only better.

The barns glow in the orange fog lights. Inside the stalls darkness swells, with an occasional flash of animal life. I hurry around them.

Farthest from the main arena is the mares' pen. I lean on the rails. The mares shy nervously, young wiry things, most of them rented for the weekend from slaughterhouses. By Sunday night, they'll be off to the slaughterhouse stockyards. I never used to think about them. I mean, what was the point?

The last few months, though, I found I couldn't watch the horse-tripping. I'd busy myself in our truck, chopping chilis, slicing onions, refilling the Coke machine, anything. But even when I'd turn away from watching the *piales en el lienzo* and *mangana a caballo, charros* performing their artistic ropework with the mares their targets, my stomach would still be tightened up because I knew how the mares would look when snared. If the *charro* does it right, the mare rolls on her shoulder, landing hard, but gets up, shaken, bruised, but walking. If he doesn't throw her correctly, she falls very hard and sometimes can't get up.

Don't get me wrong. Working the magic of the rope is hard, clever work. *Charros* are artists, as much as any writer, painter, singer, or astronomer. *Tío* Jesús trains and trains and he still screws up, snaring a mare wrong, crashing her spectacularly in a wild somersault, so she lands on her head. Sometimes the mares are so injured that the men who rented the mares started a "you broke 'em, you keep 'em" policy. If the horse is so damaged that she can't be loaded and trailered to the slaughterhouse, then they make you keep her.

I swing my leg over the top pipe and perch on the cold metal. One mare, pale as eggshells, whirls, ears up, like antennae, watching me. If she were a girl, she'd look like Fai, the Chinese girl in my class, also in the science club. Fai works long hours in her parents' Chinese takeout. Some nights, she's told me, she doesn't get to bed until two A.M. and then she has to get up at six to make it to school. Fai has deep smudges under her eyes and this little mare would, too, I bet, if horses got bags under their eyes.

I slip off the corral. Every head flings up, wild forelocks toss between pointed ears, and tension bolts up every leg. All senses lock on me, the intruder.

"Sorry," I whisper. Several mares whirl at my words and spin away across the pen to the far side. My little Chinese mare is brave. She continues to stare at me. She blinks her large, dark eyes. She shakes her neck and paws the ground with a dainty oval hoof, her gaze never shifting from my face.

Tomorrow will be different. She will burst, terrified, out of the chute. A *charro* will spur his pampered, well-groomed horse after this waif. He will snare her. He will throw her to the ground. Yes, artistically. But the ground is hard whether the rope is tossed prettily or not. In all fairness, I have to ask, is it any worse than roping calves, or goats? No. But it clutches at me with a tightness I can't ignore. I just know that I don't want to see her tomorrow frantically scrambling on her hind legs, trying to scale the arena's smooth walls, then spinning around the arena for any escape only to be slammed into the ground.

I edge away along the fence line. The wind is

MARIAN FLANDRICK BRAY

cooler, tinged with sage and damp dirt. If I was at Joshua Tree I'd train my telescope near the Hercules constellation and study M-13, a cluster of stars so dense that if you lived on a planet nearby, night would never fall. There the sky would always be filled with brilliant starlight, clusters of stars like bunches of heavy grapes, plump, white, shining.

Never would there be night. How would that change a human's life? Change a mare's life?

I unlatch the gate. A packed dirt path leads one way to the arena. Another path, softer, less used, flickers up to the riverbed. I shove the gate wide.

I think the pale mare will realize she'll need to keep going north on the riverbed to the mountains beyond the city, to a place where there is no night for her.

The mares skitter from me like bugs over a pond as I walk toward them. The starlit mare is farthest away from me, but she locks onto my gaze, telescoping the distance between us, until we are closer than any binary star system. I close in. With a quiet dignity, she suddenly folds, turns, and walks calmly out of the open gate. The other mares see her outside and trot in circles, confused. Silly things. I raise my arms, shooing them out after the pale mare.

The remaining horses rush for the gate like the tail of a comet, fine, fiery. In the lead, the pale mare trots, her tail streaming ribbons. She passes under a fog light, an alien creature, then under another and another, until she is herself again, galloping away from the grounds, traveling light.

"That's right," I say admiringly. "Don't even look back." I turn and fade away into the night as shouts from security erupt from a nearby barn. The image of the starlit mare glows before me. Maybe I won't mind as much working tomorrow because in this darkness I'm beginning to see the path the stars have laid down for me. I hurry back home, my step lighter than it has been in a long time.

The Truth in the Case of Eliza Mary Muller, by Herself

I did not want to write this. Ms. Sobol suggested it and I said no a few days ago. I have been getting mail and today I got one letter from this little girl who did not use the word *heroine*, but that is what she meant. I still do not want to write this, but I have put my hand to it and now I have to carry through, the way Daddy always said.

Daddy was Chester Nimitz Muller of Fredericksburg, Texas. He raised Sis and me about all by himself because Mama died before I was a year old. Here lately I have had three letters claiming to be from Mama, but they are all lies. My mama is in the Lutheran graveyard at Fredericksburg where she belongs. I do not know what kind of woman would write letters like the ones I am getting, but I do not want to meet her.

*   *   *

I was baptized Eliza Mary but I am called Liz, just as my big sister was baptized Sara Charlene but everyone calls her Sis. Even Bud used to call her that. She is eight years older than me and was married five years ago. Some people think that because my nephew Scooter is five years old that must be the reason she got married, but that is not true. Scooter was a premature birth. I saw him when he was born. He was too small to live, but he did anyway.

In those days Bud was a nice clean boy who worked at the 7-Eleven and passed all his classes even if he was not ever going to make honor roll. Daddy thought that seventeen was too young to get married even for a girl who grew up as fast as Sis. He thought she should go to college and see some more of the world. Sis did not care about college or the world, and she did care about Bud, so she was married and Daddy gave her away. I was a bridesmaid, which I think now was awfully nice of her because I was only nine and dirt stuck to me like paper clips to a magnet and my flowers all wilted, I hung onto them so tight. I always told her when I got married she would be my matron of honor, but now I do not think I will ever get married.

Bud and Sis moved to San Antonio right away and Bud got a building job. Daddy and I went right on living in the same house in Fredericksburg. I think

Daddy was already sick during the wedding, but the first I knew about it was two years later when he had to go to the hospital for the first time. He finally gave up smoking like Sis had always pestered him to, but it was too late, and he was in and out of hospitals the rest of his life after that.

Still he did a good job of raising me. He said if he could not see it through to the end, he would see it through as far as he could, and he did. He somewhere got the money for dancing lessons and took me hunting and fishing and taught me to cook and to tell right from wrong. When he had to go to the hospital, I would stay in San Antonio with Sis and Bud, and Sis was always real good to me, too. I cannot say we never fought, and we could not be really happy with Daddy in the hospital, but I could talk to her just the same as to Daddy. She made sure I knew everything I needed to know about boys, and when I turned eleven, she let me have a birthday party with the whole Five Palms Elementary School fifth grade.

In those days, Bud was not working regular anymore, and sometimes I would hear him and Sis fighting after I went to bed. This bothered me, but Sis told me all married people fight. Daddy said people who loved each other could always work things out, and I should mind my own business, so I did. I liked Bud fine. He would pick me up from school, and if Sis said I could not have ice cream or something he would say, "Aw, let the kid have some. Put some meat on her bones. Never could stand skinny women."

Daddy died when I was thirteen. He left all his worldly goods to me and Sis. We divided it up according to our natures and needs. For instance, Sis got the car and the washing machine, and I got the stereo and the deer rifle. It was an old stereo, but it was better than nothing. We rented out the house in Fredericksburg, the money went into the bank for my savings, and I moved in with Sis.

Bud had not worked for about six months then. "I don't believe y'all thought that out too clearly," he said to me when he picked me up from school one day. We were going straight out to get Scooter and me some new shoes, so naturally the subject of money came up. "Here's Sis and me looking after you," he said, "and you getting rent money, and you keep it all."

I had not thought about it that way before. "That doesn't sound fair," I said. "Sis is just too generous for her own good. Suppose I give her half my rent money? Two hundred dollars a month would make life a lot easier."

"It sure would," said Bud. "If I was working, I wouldn't even suggest it, but I just don't know how we'll manage till I find me a job."

So that night at dinner I said all that to her, just like it was my own idea. She looked up from wiping

Scooter's mouth and said, without even thinking about it, "No, Liz. We'll manage fine. I know that money looks like a lot now, but you wait till you want to go to college or get married, you'll see how little it amounts to."

"Now, be reasonable," said Bud. "The kid wants to pay her own way. That's fair, ain't it?"

"Not if she has to spend up her own future to do it," said Sis. They looked at each other in a hard, narrow way, like Scooter and me were not even in the room. "I can get a paper route in the morning before I go into work, and you'll find a job one of these days. Why don't you go sign up with that temporary place tomorrow?"

"Why don't you get off my back about that? I don't want to work temporary."

"It'll do till you find permanent."

"You are the most unreasonable woman that ever lived," said Bud. "Here you turn down a steady two hundred dollars a month, and then you turn around and nag at me because I won't pick up nickels and dimes."

I went and gave Scooter his bath. This was the first time they ever started fighting in front of us.

I did my best. I gave Sis all my baby-sitting money, and when the other girls went shopping I pretended I did not care. I reckon we had not got any less money than the Escobedas next door. Belia Escobeda and I used to get together with Sis's sewing machine, making clothes for Scooter and her little sister, Lisa. We were going to make our own when we got good enough, but so far we have not.

I do not like to say Bud changed. It does not seem absolutely fair and true. He did some things more often and others less, I guess. He had always had bad moods, and he had always gotten over them. You just had to be extra nice to him. Lately even when he was in a good mood with me and Scooter, he might be in a bad one with Sis. Used to be he and Sis would go out to a movie or dinner Saturday night, and I would baby-sit, but lots of Saturdays now he would go out alone and not come back till late.

Once in a while, when he came in like that, I would hear them fighting. I could not understand the words, but Scooter and I would wake up and lie there listening, and I would have to turn on the stereo or something so he would not hear. Sometimes as well as words there would be whacking noises. Next morning Bud always slept late and Sis always acted like nothing was wrong.

Then one day I came into the bedroom to borrow a good pair of hose while Sis was dressing. You know how the last clean pair always runs as soon as you put them on. Bud was sprawled out on the bed snoring with his head under his pillow. Sis was just in her slip and her bra, and I could see big bruises all up and

PENI R. GRIFFIN

down her sides. She jumped when I came in and looked at me like maybe she had done something wrong, even though I was the one who had not waited after knocking. First I felt embarrassed, so I said I was sorry, but all the time I was borrowing the hose I saw those marks. She put on her blouse and covered them.

Then I started feeling toward her the way I had started to feel toward Daddy the last couple of times he went to the hospital. Here was this person who had been looking out for me ever since I could remember, and all the time I should have been looking out for her.

I made my voice sound as much like Daddy's as I could and said, "He's got no right to do that to you. We can get him arrested."

I was kind of hoping Bud would wake up and we'd all get in a big fight and maybe solve something, but he just snored under the pillow.

"And then Scooter's daddy'll be in jail," said Sis, in what my English teacher calls a stage whisper.

"You can't just let him hit you," I said out loud. "You got to do something."

She dragged me out into the hall and shut the door behind us. "It's not as bad as it looks," she said, just like she used to say about Daddy. "I took Bud for better or worse, and right now he's got problems."

"That doesn't mean he's allowed to beat up on you!"

"Never said it did. Look, I don't say this isn't bad, but I can take it. I put my hand to this marriage, and I'm going to carry it through. If he doesn't improve once he gets a job, or if he ever lays a hand on you or Scooter, I'll divorce him so fast it'll make you dizzy, but I'm not going to just give up on him. Now you go get ready for church."

People are saying now I should have gone to a school counselor or something. I guess maybe I should have, but the idea of telling somebody whose business it was not made me sick and nervous all over. I figured Sis knew what she was doing, and the only thing I could do to help was not to leave them alone together when he was in one of his moods, if I could help it.

I could not do anything after bedtime, though. Every few weeks I would hear that going on, and I would want to run in there and stop it. I never did. One morning I did say to him, "You know, we can hear you when you come in late. Scooter needs his sleep."

He looked at me funny. I looked at the hunting calendar on the wall over his head, with the picture of the mule deer buck drinking out of the stock tank.

"Don't want to disturb my boy's rest," said Bud. "How about you, honey? You sleeping all right?"

"I'm fine," I said.

"You want me to come in and kiss you good night?" he asked, like that was funny.

I did not say anything. He was saying things like that a lot, lately.

You get four people in a two-bedroom house with only one bathroom, you are not going to have as much privacy as you would like all the time. We lived around it the best we could. For instance, when I had to move into Scooter's room, we divided it up with the chests of drawers, and were real careful and polite to each other about going into the different sides of the room. At least, we were mostly, but you cannot expect a five-year-old always to be good.

Anyway, I was used to that. Lately, Bud would do things like he wanted to embarrass me. He might come into the bathroom without knocking, or forget to close the door, or forget his clothes when he went in to shower and go traipsing around the house in a towel. Sometimes he would tease me about my figure or my boyfriends, and a couple of times he tickled me like I was still a little girl. It was all like a big joke to him, but Belia and I did not find it funny. He did this in front of Belia when I had her over, but I do not recall his ever embarrassing me in front of Sis or Scooter.

I guess now I cannot put off telling about The Day any longer. It was the last Friday before hunting season. Sis had got up all sniffly and headachey and gone to work anyway. My English teacher was out with the flu, and the sub ran out of time before she got to my oral report that I had worked on all week. Crystal Gayle was going to be downtown, and I could not afford tickets. Belia and I walked home together, and we picked up Scooter and Lisa from the kindergarten, like always. As soon as we got home they went to run wild in the yards with the Escobedas' dog.

It was one of those autumn days when it seems like the birds are all asleep or gone to Acapulco, except one lonesome grackle. The light was gray, but it was not cold much. Belia and I stood on the sidewalk and talked awhile.

I said, "If I try, I can get my homework done before I have to fix supper."

Belia said, "Mom and Dad are going out, so I got to fix supper for Lisa and put her to bed. Maybe you can come over and hear my new CDs." She had just joined a music club, and her six CDs for a penny had come in, but she had not had time to play them for me. We agreed to see each other after supper and went inside. So you see it was an ordinary day.

Bud was sitting in his chair with the stereo on. I was used to Bud being home when I came in. He claimed to do his job hunting in the morning, and who am I to say he did not? I can hear the words on the radio now as I think about it. He was listening to a station that plays songs that are several years old. That moment Moe and Joe were singing about being good old boys. I have always not liked that song. If it is supposed to poke fun at people who think a twenty-dollar football bet is a good enough reason to beat up a brother-in-law, it does not poke hard enough. Anyway, I do not know why I remember that so clearly now, because I did not notice it then. All I noticed at the time was that Bud was cleaning Daddy's deer rifle.

He had it all taken apart, with the pieces spread around, and a can of generic beer on the table next to him. When he heard the door, he looked up at me and grinned like a man with a good conscience. "Hi, Liz," he said. "Kiss a lot of boys today?"

"What are you doing with my rifle?" I asked.

He laughed like I had said something cute. "Going deer hunting. Put some meat on the table."

"I'm all for that," I said, "but I don't recall you asking if you could use my rifle."

"What do you want with a rifle?"

"Daddy left me and Sis all his worldly goods, and that rifle is part of my share," I said.

"You couldn't hit anything with it," said Bud, which was untrue and he knew it. He had eaten just as much off the whitetail I killed when I was twelve as

I had. "Don't tell me you're one of those little girls that won't share."

"If you'd asked me if you could use my gun, I'd've said yes," I said. "But you didn't have that much courtesy, did you? Where you going hunting, anyway?"

"I got friends," he said. "You mind your business and your manners. You on the rag today, or what?"

I did not answer this, but went into my half-room to do homework. The algebra did not make any sense. I do not know why anybody would want to use all those formulas, anyway. I had not done but two problems out of ten when I heard Bud come in. The radio was playing something about a man who came home drunk once too often and got locked out.

"What you want?" I asked.

"Now, you be nice to your old big brother," he said. "I just come in to be friendly." He sat down on my bed. Maybe I am inventing this, but I think I thought he was nervous about something. Like he wanted to ask me for something.

"I got homework to do," I said.

"You got all weekend for that."

"No time like the present."

"Now, don't talk like that, or you'll grow up like your sister."

"Sounds good to me." I wrote down an answer and looked at it. It did not look right.

"That's because you ain't married to the frigid —" I will not write out what he called her. It made me jump up and look at him. He was sprawled out on my bed like he owned it, getting his greasy hair on my panda bear, which is as big as a pillow and does just as well.

"Don't you talk about Sis that way!" I shouted at him.

He lolled there, grinning. "Talk how I please in my own house."

"Your house? How can it be your house? Sis pays all the rent and buys all the groceries and pays all the bills. I bring more money into this house from baby-sitting than you ever have since I got here."

"It's my house," he said, "and my family and my gun in my gun cabinet, and I can do what I want to."

Right then is when I said what I should not have. "Like beating up on your wife? Yeah, that sure makes you a big shot."

He sat up and grabbed hold of my arm. It hurt. He put his face right up next to mine and said to me, "That ain't none of your business."

I used to play-wrestle with Daddy, but Bud was lots stronger. "You turn me loose right now," I said. I did not like the way he looked at me, especially not from so close. I was even a little scared, but I am not sure of what. You will think I am stupid, but I had never thought of him hurting me, only Sis. "Sis said if you ever laid a hand on me or Scooter she'd divorce you, and then where'll you be?"

"You ain't going to tell, you little tease," he said, and did something with his free hand that I'd rather not talk about. "Not before I tell her all about how you been trying to vamp me."

Which was a dead lie; but I guess you know that. Sis would have, too. It did not scare me. His breath in my face did. By now I had figured out what was in his mind. "Leave go!" I said, and kicked him. Not like they do in the movies, which I think is tacky, but just on the shin.

I do not remember, or anyway I do not want to, all the things he said to me, and about me, and about Sis. He was not a bit like the same man that used to buy me ice cream. He said some things to me that I try hard to forget and certainly will not mark up good paper with. One thing he did say was that Sis could divorce him, but she could not get rid of him. He had rights to Scooter. That this man was Scooter's daddy and could see him any time he pleased did not seem right to me.

Bud was not drunk. They say you would have to drink till you drowned to get real drunk on that generic beer. If he had been drunk, I do not think I would have been so scared.

PENI R. GRIFFIN

I got loose from him and ran into the living room, meaning to run out and lock myself in next door with Belia and Scooter and Lisa. He got ahead of me and started chasing me around the house. I do not like to think what would have happened if Sis had not gotten off early with the first stage of the flu that day.

She came in on us in the kitchen right after he tore the buttons off my blouse. She waded in and smashed Bud on the nose with her fist. He dropped me. "This is it!" she screamed in his face. "You get out of this house right now! Tonight!"

"Shut up!" he roared, and called her a filthy name. He ignored me, grabbed her hair, and started hitting on her. The sounds were just like the ones from the bedroom late Saturday nights. The radio was playing "I Never Promised You a Rose Garden," a song I used to like a whole lot.

Sis did not scream or cry. Instead, she hit back. I picked myself up off the floor. Before I could think what to do I saw Scooter, standing in the back door. He just stood there with the wide gray sky behind him, looking at his dad beating on his mom; and his mom trying to get loose and hit back; and his aunt with her blouse all torn up. His eyes were round and black, like a Raggedy Andy.

Suddenly I was real calm. I went to Scooter, standing between him and that sight he never should have seen. "Scooter," I said, in the kind of voice you

THE TRUTH IN THE CASE OF ELIZA MARY MULLER, BY HERSELF

STAY TRUE **123**

have to use to get a five-year-old to obey you, "Scooter, listen up." He turned those Raggedy Andy eyes all the way up to my face. "Scooter, you go next door and tell Belia to call the police. Go on, now. Quick!"

Somebody was burning leaves. I remember the smell. Scooter stared at me. Just then Bud said something particularly nasty to Sis — something a boy of five could not have understood, but said loud and mean. Scooter turned around and hightailed it across the yard. I locked the door after him.

I walked past Sis and Bud. They did not look at me. Sis was trying to knock him over by wrapping her legs around him, but one thing Daddy did not teach us was fighting. Her face was all wet. He was not hitting just her sides anymore, but anyplace he could get at, which was most of her. He had her bent over and held pretty tight with her arms behind her back.

I walked on into the living room. Bud had put Daddy's gun back in the cabinet, but the keys were still out on the coffee table. I took out Daddy's rifle and a box of ammunition. I can remember every name he called her while I loaded it. I went back into the kitchen and stuck the barrel up next to his face. It got his attention. He did not let go, but he stopped hitting.

"You turn her loose and get out of this house," I said, "or else I'll shoot you dead."

PENI R. GRIFFIN

He looked at me like maybe I had fallen from the moon. "Sure, Liz," he said. "You do that!"

He was not supposed to say that. I had not expected him to. He should have known that once I set my hand to that gun, I had to carry it through.

I do not guess the mess would have bothered a soldier, but it sure bothered us. I kept throwing up. Even after nothing was left in my stomach, even after Sis got all the stuff washed off both of us, I could still see and smell and feel it all, and I would throw up again. Sometimes now when I have to cook dinner in that kitchen I still throw up.

Sis locked the kitchen so as not to disturb the scene of the crime. She cleaned me off and sat with me in the bathroom till the police came. She wanted to clean off the gun and say she had done it, but I said, "What about Scooter?" Of course she saw at once that lying to protect me would be the worst thing for Scooter, and me, too, in the long run. Where could we go but a foster home?

The police and the courthouse people have all been very kind. The newspapers have not been, but I guess they cannot help it. I never thought about it before, but a newspaper's job is to poke into other people's business. I do not know what we would have done without the Escobedas to keep all the curious people, the reporters and the souvenir hunters, away from us. Ghouls, Ms. Sobol calls them. Ms.

Sobol is the lawyer the city is paying to take care of me.

Ms. Sobol says there is not much chance of my going to jail or even reform school. She says I did not commit a crime, just a mistake in judgment. A mistake in judgment that kills a man is enough like a crime to me. I see our name and all the things I did not want to talk to the school counselor about dragged in the newspaper dirt, and I see our house on TV, and I think of other ways I could have coped with Bud, but it is too late now.

And here this little girl writes and thinks I am a heroine. I am not a bit sorry I pulled the trigger. That was Bud's fault. I am sorry I said that thing that made him so mad, and I am sorry I picked up the gun, but the rest of it I could not do anything about once those two things were done. I did what I had to do, and some of what I had to do was wrong.

And that's the whole truth about all of it.

The Statue of Liberty Factory

The main thing about this story happened in 1977, but it really mostly started one night in 1975 when we were watching Walter Cronkite and there was all this stuff about how the Bicentennial in '76 was going to be so HISTORIC and there was this long tracking shot from a helicopter of the Statue of Liberty in New York Harbor and my mother said, "That's what I'll do."

Nina and Toby were smashing their Tonkas into the front of the couch near my feet (*rrr-rrr-rrr-KKKKK!*) and Dad's feet, too, and Nina actually clipped Dad's ankle. He let out a sort of *erk* and went on reading the paper, which he always does when the news is on: a two-for-one deal.

"It's perfect, perfect," Mom went on. She grabbed a piece of paper and began sketching the

Statue of Liberty, making all kinds of notes and diagrams around it, when from out in the kitchen there was this really big crash and Mom said, "Where's MiniMac?" without *actually* looking up from her drawing because we didn't hear any crying.

I went out to the kitchen. MiniMac had pulled the tablecloth off the kitchen table, and the lazy Susan with the napkin holder and the salt and pepper and the sugar bowl and some cereal box toys and a bunch of other stuff, including a really dried-out-looking lemon and A SMASHED PLATE HE WAS ABOUT TO EAT A PIECE OF, were on the floor in front of him, and I could tell he also needed changing, so I took the piece of plate away, took him upstairs, and figured someone else could clean up the kitchen 'cause there had to be somebody else in this house who would notice.

That was the night Mom got her great idea about making the souvenirs for the Bicentennial (she's an artist *plus* she has a business degree), and our house turned into THE STATUE OF LIBERTY FACTORY.

See, this was the thing. You know those little marionette kind of toys that are jointed and have elastic inside them and they're on a little stand with a button underneath and when you push the button, the figure's arm waves, or it bows, or something. I always make them totally crumple, and then stand right up.

Crumple. Stand up. Crumple. Stand up. That's how I like to do it.

So Mom designed a push-button puppet of the Statue of Liberty. She didn't actually make them herself. She just designed it and made a model out of this plastic clay material, and then got this factory in Bridgeport (Premier Molding and Extruding, Inc.) to manufacture them, and she took them to stores in New York City (even Bloomingdale's), and they bought TONS of them.

As you can imagine, we also had tons of them all over the house. Say you open the broom closet, there's the Statue of Liberty standing between Lemon Pledge and Mr. Clean, holding up her torch like she's supposed to be a night-light. Or you go looking for the slide projector so you can practice monologues in front of a spotlight, and there's a dozen of them with their pointy crowns staring at you from on top of "Michigan Camping Trip — 1965."

I got kind of interested in it, too, the real thing I mean, because it's pretty interesting, how the people of France gave it to the United States in 1886, and how tall it is and how many steps and all that, and THEN I found out about THE POEM written on it by some woman named Emma Lazarus and that really blew my mind and I started memorizing it and reciting it all over the house.

GIVE ME YOUR TIRED, YOUR POOR,
YOUR HUDDLED MASSES YEARNING TO
    BREATHE FREE,
THE WRETCHED REFUSE OF YOUR
    TEEMING SHORE.
SEND THESE, THE HOMELESS, TEMPEST-
    TOST TO ME.
I LIFT MY LAMP BESIDE THE GOLDEN
    DOOR!

REALLY dramatic, that's how I would read it as I lifted my lamp (usually a hairbrush or an ice cream cone, whatever), and Dad would groan from underneath the twins and say something like, "Send these, the toothless, the tempest-tossed —" and bounce the twins right off him so they would scream and you could see their gums where their baby teeth were falling out practically every week. Or Roger, IF he came home after school, would stand staring into the refrigerator in his completely ripped Led Zeppelin T-shirt saying, "Talk about your wretched refuse. Grotesque." And MiniMac would bang a Statue of Liberty with his plastic hammer. The Statue of Liberty Factory, see?

But the thing is, Mom really made a lot of money from those button puppets, when the Bicentennial actually happened, and so we had what they call a rise in our standard of living, but it didn't really change things in our house that much, although Mom opened pretty big savings accounts for all of us and told us when we were sixteen we could do ANYTHING WE WANTED with our money, and when I said, "Like get to go to Paris for the summer and play my guitar on the Boulevard Saint-Michel?" she said, "Sure, you bet."

So that's the whole background, and Mom continued making these push-button puppets of different national monuments like the Washington Monument (kind of boring, just an obelisk toppling over), Golden Gate Bridge (a little too much like an example of what an earthquake might do), the Empire State Building (she put a King Kong on the deluxe collector's edition), and they were all really popular, and this spring of '77 when the story REALLY begins, she was trying to design a puppet of Mount Rushmore. It was pretty complicated, and through an open window we could hear the twins and MiniMac hollering about something and the phone rang a lot for Mom on business, so it wasn't excellent timing when I looked up from reading the liner notes on *Hotel California* and said, "So, Mom, now that I'm sixteen, this is the summer I'm going to Paris."

And Mom said, "So, Monica, now that you're sixteen, you must be out of your mind."

So the argument was EPIC, and Nina and Toby

and MiniMac actually climbed up a tree to watch us through the window screaming at each other about how "you said I could," and "I need you around this summer, Monica," and "This is like living in a third world dictatorship!" and then MiniMac actually FELL OUT OF THE TREE and the twins started screaming and Mom rushed outside yelling, "You see! You see why I need you?"

I took it up with Judge MacAllister, aka BigMac, aka Dad, and he just said, "Monica, if your mother says no, it's no."

And all I could do was look really haughty and say, "My name is Monique," and walk with great dignity up to my room and shut the door very quietly, and then scream at the top of my lungs. Roger started banging on the wall. "AS IF YOU CAN REALLY HEAR ME WITH BAD COMPANY BLARING SO LOUD!" I screamed back.

So I sat on my bed and picked up my guitar and stared at this picture of Jackson Browne I had traced from an album cover and then opened my door and yelled down the stairs, "I LIVE AMONG POLITICAL SAVAGES" and shut the door again and picked up the guitar, which always helped me think, or at least look really pensive and thoughtful.

What I was thinking about was how at school everyone had become so political that spring, and we had sit-ins to protest all kinds of things, like when our

JENNIFER ARMSTRONG

field day was canceled because some boys put a VW Bug on the gym roof, stuff like that. I wanted to stage a sit-in to protest my parents turning traitors on me, but a sit-in with one person wouldn't be that OVER-WHELMING, even if I got MiniMac to sit with me for a while by reading to him.

I had a push-button puppet of the Statue of Liberty hanging by her neck from the light cord over my bed (which always made Mom give me a dirty look), and I reached for it and made it go crumple, stand up, crumple, stand up, and I had this BRILLIANT idea, which I put into action the next morning.

First of all, I hasten to add (with one finger in the air, the way our neighbor, Mrs. Brillstein, does it), this was not just spoiled brat behavior on my part. We have COUSINS in Paris. Not even second cousins, they're FIRST cousins. Dad's brother, Lewis, married a French lady, Aunt Claudette, and they have two kids, Richard and Paul (also twins, by the way) and they live in Paris, so it wasn't as though I'd be going to Paris and LIVING ON THE STREETS AND BEGGING FOR BREAD AND BEING AP-PROACHED BY STRANGE FRENCH MEN.

And second of all, it was obvious that my mother was simply angling for a handy baby-sitter for the summer, and that she hadn't even considered Roger, who, although an idiot, was more or less capable of keeping the house from burning down with the twins and MiniMac inside. Just because I was the only person in the house who took care of anything on a regular basis didn't mean I was the only person CAPABLE of it.

FURTHERMORE (also with my finger in the air, the way Mrs. Brillstein does it), I considered it beneath my dignity to do a lot of wheedling and bargaining and coming up with good reasons. No CULTURAL AND ARTISTIC TREASURES, none of this BROADENING MY HORIZONS, not a word of INVALUABLE EXPERIENCE. Why should I take such a basically weak position? My parents had agreed earlier that I could go to Paris when I was sixteen, and they had reneged. We're talking about a principle.

So I was justified in what I did.

And this is what it was.

When I went down to breakfast that morning, I was dressed in a very well-draped and pinned gray sheet, with a tinfoil crown of pointy rays, and I held a book and a torch (flashlight, that is). Toast paused on the way to mouths, coffee cups remained poised in the air, milk dribbled from the Lucky Charms spoons as I nodded hello to my family at the breakfast table, took a banana, and made my way out the door.

"What's she doing?" or variations of that question bubbled up from the breakfast table and were cut off as the door shut behind me. Outside, robins jabbed at the grass and miscellaneous other birds twittered and cheeped. Across the street, Mr. Brillstein was walking down to the sidewalk in his slippers to get his *Times*. I heard him mutter, "*Oy gevalt*," when he saw me, but I waved and smiled, and then took up my position on the walk that leads to our front door.

Imitating the Statue of Liberty is easy. Really. It is very easy to do. You hold your book in one hand, raise your flashlight into the air in the other, and stare straight ahead. It's HOLDING that pose for a long time that's hard, but I knew that going in, don't get me wrong. After about five minutes I heard a muffled sort of thump and bump and faint clicking of curtain rings at the window behind me, so I turned around to see Nina and Toby and MiniMac looking at me with their noses squished against the window. They stared at me. Then they disappeared. I went back to staring straight ahead.

After a while, Dad opened the front door and strolled out, lighting a cigarette. He threw the match away and looked at me for a moment.

"So, what's this all about?"

"Protest."

"Protest for what?"

"For going to Paris."

"Your mother says you aren't going."

"I say I am."

"She says otherwise."

"So that's her opinion."

Dad smoked and looked at the Brillsteins' house. My flashlight arm was beginning to tire.

"How long are you planning to do this protesting?"

"Until you and Mom keep your promise."

"Oh."

He chucked his cigarette away and went inside. I stood there looking over at the Brillsteins' while the cigarette burned itself out on the grass. Birds chirped some more. The door opened again and Mom came out.

"This is foolish, Monica."

"I beg to differ."

"It's a school day. How long are you planning to stand here?"

"Until you and Dad keep your promise."

"You cut school, it's on your permanent record."

I should add here that Mom doesn't usually talk like a vice principal. This is how I knew I was getting somewhere.

The Brillsteins' door opened and Mr. Brillstein came out, swinging his briefcase. "Good morning! So, Halloween already?"

"Just a misunderstanding," Mom explained, calling across the street.

"It's a protest, Mr. Brillstein. I'm going to imitate the Statue of Liberty until I gain my own liberty."

Our neighbor cocked his head, birdlike. "You're a prisoner, Monica?"

"It's just a misunderstanding," Mom said again.

"It's a political protest, Mr. Brillstein."

A car drove by and slowed down to look at me, then sped up. Mr. Brillstein cocked his head the other way, also birdlike. "Political action. That's good in a young person. Have a nice day," and he got in his Caddy and backed down the driveway with a wave.

Mom went inside. A few minutes later, Roger slouched down the driveway on the way to the bus stop. He didn't even look at me, but that was typical. A few minutes after that, Dad drove away. I wanted to switch arms with the flashlight, but that wouldn't have been right, so I didn't. After a while, Mom and MiniMac walked Nina and Toby to the elementary school bus stop. When Mom and MiniMac came back up the driveway, Mom ignored me.

"Hi, Mo-ca," MiniMac said.

"Hi, Mini, come here a second, okay?"

He came over, and I got him to hold my flashlight up for a few minutes so I could go to the bathroom. Then I stood there on the front walk for the rest of the morning. Mom brought me a sandwich at noon but didn't say anything. I recited some soliloquies, some poems, stuff like that, including the Statue of Liberty poem, you know:

GIVE ME YOUR TIRED, YOUR POOR,
YOUR HUDDLED MASSES YEARNING TO
   BREATHE FREE,
THE WRETCHED REFUSE OF YOUR
   TEEMING SHORE.
SEND THESE, THE HOMELESS, TEMPEST-
   TOST TO ME.
I LIFT MY LAMP BESIDE THE GOLDEN
   DOOR!

Only our front door wasn't golden, it was red. Around two-thirty, a car pulled up and some friends pried themselves out.

"Monica, this is great."

"No nukes, man."

"Free the POWs."

"Earth Power."

"This is about Paris," I explained.

My friends were checking out my costume, clicking my flashlight on and off. Debra Harvell was rearranging my hair under my crown, sticking it behind my years. "Paris? Cool."

"You're homework for social studs, you know."

That shocked me. "For real?"

"For real."

"Like a report and everything."

After a few more minutes of that, they all left. I

JENNIFER ARMSTRONG

felt somewhat pleased with myself. I mean, permanent records are one thing, but being homework is really something entirely different. At about four-thirty (I think, I'm not sure, I wasn't wearing a watch, but the twins had come home by then), a guy from the local paper came and took my picture, and I told him a lot of stuff about how UNFAIR it was, and why this was a legitimate political protest, and then he went away. The twins and MiniMac used me as a base in this complicated tag game they were playing. They bumped into me a lot, but I was still keeping my pose, even though I was ACHING all over. I pictured myself being one of Mom's Statue of Liberty puppets, and having someone push the button under my feet that would make me crumple to the ground, all limp. Dad waved when he came home.

"Hey, kiddo."

"Hi, Dad."

"Still protesting?"

"Still protesting."

"Planning to sleep outside?"

"I've got a torch."

"Right."

So I did. I actually did stay outside with the flashlight on. It was a warm night, so that was okay, and it wasn't my imagination that a lot of people drove slowly down the street, coming to see if it was true that one of the MacAllister kids was really imitating the Statue of Liberty on the front lawn, and sure enough, there I was all right. I finally lay down and got into the correct pose flat on the ground, and wrapped my sheet around me, and I slept that way.

"You're in the paper!" Roger called from the front door that morning.

I knew that already, since the paper had landed on my face at six o'clock and I'd read it with my flashlight. I was stiff all over, but my resolve was equally firm. I would not crumple.

"Monica, you've made your point, come inside."

"Can I go to Paris like you said I could, Mom?"

There was a very meaningful silence from her. She went inside and shut the door instead of answering.

A little while later, a TV truck pulled up in front of the house, and a reporter and a camera guy and a microphone guy walked up the path to me.

"Morning, Miss Liberty."

"Morning."

"Mind if I ask you a few questions?"

I glanced behind me. The whole family was standing in the front door: Mom, Dad, Roger, Nina, Toby, and MiniMac. MiniMac was playing with a Statue of Liberty push-button puppet. He was doing the thing I always do. Crumple. Stand up. Crumple. Stand up.

"Go ahead."

Mom was watching what MiniMac was doing. I held my flashlight even higher as the camera guy switched on his light.

"I understand you're planning to stand here in imitation of the Statue of Liberty until your parents let you go to Paris. Can you give me some background?"

MiniMac was still at it. Crumple. Stand up. Crumple. Stand up.

"One year ago, my parents agreed that I could go to Paris when I turned sixteen. I have turned sixteen, and they have welched. Simple as that."

"Is that a punishment for something you did?"

"Nope. Just a punishment for no good reason."

"And you believe that by imitating the Statue of Liberty you will change their minds?"

"I'm trying to prove a point, here. Sticking to my guns, you know? I will not crumble."

"Not trying to get into the record books or something?"

"Nope. I'm trying to get into Paris, France."

I turned around and gave Mom a MEANING-FUL STARE.

Mom gave me one, too.

And then she said, "Oh, for goodness' sake, all right!"

I took the Statue of Liberty toy MiniMac was playing with and threw it up into the air so hard that it ACTUALLY VANISHED! I mean, we do have a lot of trees around and everything, and it might have gotten stuck, but my thought was I might have thrown it hard enough to send it back to the people of France with thanks for having sent it to us in the first place.

And I would be right behind it.

Stay True

We chose the hill back of Sycamore Woods beside the swamp because the grown-ups — *groans,* as we called them — never came back there. Mosquitoes. Groans hate mosquitoes worse than they hate pizza on a sofa. Or at least about the same. So we made the dirt-run down there. We didn't want to get contaminated by groan molecules.

I remember pounding down the path making smooth dirt cement with my sneakers. I dragged the treads off my shoes all through April and May to have them smooth and ready for dirt-sliding. By August we'd be gliding through goldenrod.

"We" was me and Baby Don-Don, who's big now but he was named after his daddy, Big Don, and since he was zero years old we've always called him Baby. I think it's about the dumbest thing on earth to name a whole different person after your same old self, but that's the way some people are. I hope I have a baby boy some day. I'll name him after me, his mama. That'd show people just how dumb I think "same naming" is.

Anyway there was Baby Don-Don, Checked-Wheat, Stick-Person-Girl, and me, Molly-be-Gone. Stick-Person-Girl was so skinny we figured she'd never have breasts. It was hard to tell she was a girl, which is why we added Girl to her name. And Checked-Wheat ate cereal a lot, so I guess his name came from that, but I don't really remember.

I was Molly-be-Gone because either the groans wished I was gone or they were looking around for me and shouting about how gone I was. And I liked that fine. I liked being gone from groans.

I was Molly-be-Gone most of my summer life. But summer life never goes on as long as I could live it. September always comes *whooshing* in like that big old butterfly net hanging in the shed. You're flying around in the sun without shoes or equations and then, *whomp,* September sweeps down over you, and you're in a jar being studied.

I don't know who thought up school, except of course it was groans. The whole idea of squeezing large numbers of kids into one building and then dividing us up by what year we were born is as dumb as singing "the cradle will fall" to a baby. I've been squeezed into rooms with most of the same kids practically my whole life and I've never learned one good thing from it. I mean school is not the place for young minds. It seems more like the place you might want to go if you were old, worn out, and just needed somewhere to slump.

When I start going back over all those years in elementary, middle, and now high school and I try thinking of the good stuff, it's mostly not school. It's those summers in between or a book I read when I was supposed to be *school learning*. It's gluing the boy's toilet seats down and not getting caught. Or passing notes to Stick-Person-Girl before she got breasts and got too cool.

I tell you, school makes girls crazy. It tears best friends apart. Like Stick-Person-Girl and me. We used to not care what those idiot boys did. We would not have cared if they'd strapped booster rockets to their butts and shot off the planet. But now. Now! It seems like most girls, especially Stick-Person, have lost themselves to boy games. And boy games make you act as if mosquitoes sucked your brains out your ears.

I try to keep myself safe from the boy-crazies. It's not that hard, but I'm proud of it. I don't know why I know better than all those perfect-haired girls. Maybe because I let my mind stretch in open spaces like Sycamore Woods. Or maybe it's books. Maybe that's why.

I mean I've been to so many places in books and in my mind, I'm not scared that high school is my whole life. I can tell it's more like a bad zit that stays too long. But you know it'll go away. It'll disappear and you won't even remember where it was. I figure high school's kind of like that. But not caring about not being cool is not cool and not being cool can ruin a lot of things when you're stuck in high school jail for most of your day.

Every day when our sentence is up and they open the gates, I head for Sycamore Woods to air out my brains. I have this tree in there, a hollow old sycamore, that's my own private studio. I hide in there when I need my own place to be. One Wednesday after school, I was hanging out in my tree when I heard whispering.

"Pull the petals off seventeen daisies without breathing in between, and don't get mixed on the 'loves me and loves me nots', and then you'll know."

That's weird Nell Weems! I said to myself. I'd recognize that tight know-what's-right voice anywhere.

"That's weird, Nell Weems," said Stick-Person-Girl right back at her.

"Well it's the only sure way I know for you to find out, short of asking Tim Swane."

"Forget that," said Stick-Person. "Tim Swane would beat it back to Skyler so fast I may as well just print it on the Dairy Queen billboard: RUTH ROOTS

DESPERATE TO KNOW IF SKYLER DREMLER LOVES HER. CALL 555-3991 WITH INFORMATION."

I couldn't believe my sorry ears! Stick-Person-Girl, alias Ruth Roots, listening to Nell Weems! The idea that Stick-Person would choose to listen to the words of Nell Weems over me made me as mad as squashed wasps.

"Well, Ruth Roots, you're just going to turn into a mashed potato lump if you don't get on with it," said Nell. "There's daisies back of Marshes' barn — I saw them yesterday morning. They're caked in cow pies, but we can find some that aren't cruddy."

"So I pluck those petals off and end with 'loves me not,'" said Stick-Person, "and then what? I march on over to Skyler's house and yell, 'Marshes' barn daisies say you don't love me, so I'm going to Homecoming with Steven Russell and serves you right?'"

I almost snorted right out my nose. I do that sometimes when I'm trying not to laugh. Nell Weems just kept right on.

"Ruth, you just get ahead of yourself all day long. You probably know your back better than your front."

"Well, I like knowing before I get to a place," said Stick-Person-Girl. "But I guess destroying daisy petals is something to do."

And that was as much of the conversation as I heard down there in Sycamore Woods. They beat themselves back on up the path leading away from me — away from their salvation.

I think the person who invented daisy petals spent too long in a catnip patch. No way you're ever going to get to know anything about true love from cow pies and daisies.

And more to the point, no boy on this planet knows what he wants, and certain for sure no boy in our high school. Unless he's an alien and landed from someplace else. I mean boys think they want their physicals rubbed and touched by female skin, but that's not the kind of information you want to go basing your life on. You sure as mud can't be looking to no boys for no answers to no thing. And that's my final word on that.

Well anyway, Stick-Person-Girl and those daisies. When Stick-Person got too big to play with me — lost her stick parts and got breasts and boys — she lost her mind, too. Daisies! That's just the kind of thing your mind starts doing if you let it run around with boy thoughts for too long.

I'd have laughed at them if it weren't for one thing. I missed Stick-Person-Girl. The truth is I knew she still had brains in there if she could just get the part of her head that goes gloopy over boys flushed out.

And worse, I missed being best friends. Ever since

back when we hit ninth grade, she'd been racing away from me with her new friends — the ones who walked wobbly from having to keep their look-good-hair staying good. It seemed like every new day she had new makeup on her face or new hair or new clothes until she just plain vanished. Now Stick-Person can't even walk down the hallway straight anymore — has to check herself and scan for boy creatures.

It's like a strange girl's wearing Stick-Person's outsides. We used to spend long times writing down our brilliant ideas and wonder-abouts, our minds electric and shooting sparks. We shared everything — dreams, fears, lunch. . . . Now I hardly knew if she had real thoughts anymore.

But the very next day in English class, Mr. Hoonan handed me back Stick-Person's notebook by mistake. I spent my whole lunch hour reading everything she'd written in there, every word. I'm nosy, who cares, but she writes real good. And I missed her, so this was like hanging out again.

You wouldn't know it from her lipstick and hip dancing, but she thinks things. That lunch hour I read pages and pages of powerful thoughts. And I saw her soul again. One bunch of words said:

DISAPPEARING

My hair skims my shoulders.
I swing my head
and strands sweep my face
or catch in the corner of my mouth.
I toss my bangs like a horse.
I toss them gently and make my face blank,
like I don't notice.
But I'm thinking, Did that look good?
  Did he notice?

We stand in a line in front of the mirror brushing.
Brushing and brushing our hair and talking.
Talking as fast as we brush. As hard as we brush.
We talk about nothing. Boys. Other girls.

Everything I do to make myself bigger
shrinks my insides small. I'm scared
that one day I'll check the mirror
and I'll be gone.

Stick-Person-Girl was still in there and I figured I'd better get her out.

That night I got to thinking again about her wrecking daisies. It didn't seem right. Her inside mind was too good for scraping cow crud off daisy petals, so I hated to see her outside self do it. Like go-

C. DREW LAMM

ing to some dance with some boy means squat in the universe. I mean if it happens, all right, but when girls start squatting in cow pies just to get to dances, someone's got to slap the universe around and change that. So that night I went to bed in my clothes.

Just like Cinderella only backwards, when the clock struck twelve I put on both shoes and headed away from home. I had work to do. First off I thought maybe Skyler Romance Dremler needed a change of hairstyles. I had the right equipment. Three tubes of glue, elastic bands, pink bows, and scissors, just in case. Skyler had the perfect tree right outside his bedroom window. I'd heard him bragging about it being like his own private entrance. So that's what I did — I entered!

I don't know how I knew I could perform such a delicate operation without waking Skyler up, but I think I knew it so hard I made it happen. That boy slept like a hog after downing three troughs of slop.

I braided most of his cool hair, added the pink bows, and then cemented it all with glue — the kind that sticks tight and won't wash out no matter what. My only fear was that he'd get stuck to his pillowcase. But that could be thoughtful of me really — give him something to hide his big old head in.

The last thing I did was cut off any pieces of hair that fell out of the braids. It left patches, but those extra hairs looked messy sticking out. I finished up and walked right out his front door — like I'd made a call or been invited over to renovate Skyler.

That done, I slept good — felt like a wild fairy godmother messing with the prince. It's not like I was trying to punish Skyler for having Stick-Person go all loose brains over him. He just needed to know that he'd better try on a few new things other than just cool hair and an okay face. It sure wouldn't hurt him none to have to figure out a few new ways to be liked. I mean I don't know as you can take much credit for having hair that's neat and a face that's smooth. So probably it was like a good thing I was doing for Skyler.

But what I really wanted was for Stick-Person-Girl to remember the underneath parts, like in her writing. And it didn't seem she was going there without help. She was too flop-hearted over the way Skyler's butt tucked above his legs and how his hair fell after he hand-combed it. This was just going to be one great big old opportunity for everyone to get their priorities straight.

Next day I was early for school. I didn't care about getting all the glory for my great idea. I just wanted to be there to see it arrive. The thing about Skyler's parents is that they don't let Skyler skip out of school for no reason. He can be dragging on his knees sick and they send him in. So, they were on my

C. DREW LAMM

side. And sure enough I saw Skyler's car heading slowlike down the street in front of the school right as the last bell was ringing.

One thing about our school is, no hats. That's always made me mad up until that day. I was learning. Learning how to turn life to my advantage. So up drives Skyler and he's got no hair! It's gone. And that boy has got one smooth head. You could see his eyes like sparks, daring you to say it, daring you to look anywhere above his eyebrows.

"Nice head," I said as he marched past me.

He stopped dead and shot those spark eyes at me. And then you know what that boy creature did? He laughed. Right there on his way up the steps to school hell, he laughed.

"Yeah," he said. "Always knew my head shape was the best part. Didn't you?"

I tried to breathe normal and said, "Why'd you do it?"

He stared hard and then shrugged.

"Why not?" he said and swung in those doors.

Damn he was good. I never figured he'd be that good. I mean I know no boy is going to show up to school in pink bows, and if I could've done it during study hall, I would've. I *guess* I knew no boy is going to walk two feet with bows, but I just hoped that glue would take away those kind of choices.

But worse than no bows, I spent every hall moment that day looking for Skyler. Instead of walking the halls free and independent in my mind, I kept sliding looks at Skyler. You'd have thought he was more interesting than my own life.

All day long he was surrounded by guys whacking him, laughing and being cool. And the girls did outer rings smiling and looking all amazed like Skyler has the best ideas they ever saw. Skyler was this school hero. He was walking brave. His new head said, "Yeah right, make me, just try to stop me." It was the perfect insult to the no-boys'-hair-below-the-shoulders rule. Who could touch him? They couldn't make him grow it back 'til it did.

And the thing is, *I* got to believing he was brilliant. Someone'd say to me, "Man, can you believe Skyler thought of that?" And I'd just stand there amazed and shaking my head, "No, I can not." I'd even laughed at one of his jokes and looked to see if he noticed. I started thinking he didn't look so bad being naked above the eyebrows.

It wasn't 'til I got myself out those doors, away from there and into Sycamore Woods, that I started thinking real again. I had lost and I hadn't even noticed. I'd succumbed to boy power. Just like Stick-Person-Girl!

I felt my insides blowing up and shoving my brains right out of my head. The girl-crazies rushed in on me, and I felt like Stick-Person must feel when you can't walk straight anymore without looking around.

Here I was in my woods. In my place of worship and free thoughts, and I had Skyler ruining my head. I had Skyler running into my thoughts slowing me down. I started thinking about what I might wear to school tomorrow and that's when I got madder than hail. I got so mad at Skyler Dremler I cried real tears. I hadn't cried real tears since Wilbur Force, my dog, died. But I felt like something had died. Some brave and separate part of me had died. The part that could see clear and run free and not care had died. I'd cut it right out with Skyler's hair.

I was going to have to vow to myself that I would not under any circumstances fill up my mind with "what-to-wear thoughts," and I could not believe it. I could not believe I had to take time for this.

"Boys are devastation," I shouted. I shouted it real loud just to make it true. To make it stick in me. And that's when Skyler Dremler appeared. I swear I don't know what he was doing creeping around in my space, but he peered into the trunk of my tree and found me.

"You run wild in these woods?" he said. "They should put up signs warning people."

I just stared. Me with the mouth like Meuller's Stream that keeps on running words through the air even when I'm sleeping. I just stared. I stared at him like he was a vacuum that had sucked out my insides.

"I'm locking my window tonight so I don't wake up with permanent ink on my head tomorrow," he said.

I just gawked some more until finally he walked away.

I slumped down inside the trunk and stared at my knees. I couldn't even yell stuff at him in my mind. I was running on empty. And I was scared. It was like having aliens take over my body. I knew real well the girl I'd been and grown up with. I could anticipate rough spots and smooth them over before I wrecked myself. I looked after myself real good. But now this! Here I was in the middle of my sanctuary, my woods, being struck dumb not by thunder above the pines or a hawk plummeting from the sky, but by a mere boy. I'd been skewered by a boy with no hair.

I needed straightening as much as Stick-Person-Girl. I see trees as giant hairbrushes. Or brain brushes really. Because most times when I go into the woods and my mind is all tatters and knots, those trees brush me smooth. I can feel them hard-stroking my brains, untangling and freeing my mind. And when I leave, I'm in place. So I climbed out, stepped away from my tree, and just looked up as far as I could for as long as I could and made myself and my tangles small. The sky high above and those branches reaching wide made my brains like a pearl in my palm, and they weren't so heavy to carry around. I walked out ready to revolt.

First thing I did next day at school was to find Stick-Person-Girl.

"I don't think reading other people's private thoughts is legal or anything but when Mr. Hoonan handed me your book by mistake after English class it was kind of like permission. Like a hall pass into your notebook. So I went in."

Stick-Person had been flicking her hair, looking around and through me the whole time she did it, sort of like I was an annoying stop light on a day she was in a hurry. Like she was just waiting for the light to change and she'd be gone. But instead of the light turning green, she turned red.

"I have my notebook," she said.

"You have *my* notebook," I said.

She scrambled around in her book bag and dragged out the marbled purple notebook we'd both chosen for English. She knew as soon as she saw it. I knew she would. She's like me. Knows every scratch on the purple, knows where the spiral part's been squashed. If she hadn't been watching Skyler with every hair on her scalp, she'd have known when Mr. Hoonan handed it back. Like I'd known.

"Why do you let Skyler make you act so stupid? You used to be smart," I said.

STAY TRUE

She hated me then. She'd been prancing around in her head wearing a diamond dress and then I walked up with a mirror. And there she was in old rags and she knew I was right. She knew she was letting boys mess with her life. But she hated being told. She hated being reminded that I knew her. Knew her deep down well. She walked away from me so fast I felt a breeze.

That night a yowling sound came slipping out from behind Sycamore Woods. I kept saying, "Owls, owls, it's just owls," but I knew no owl made a sound like that. I sat inside the screen door all froze up inside. All froze. All hot. The sound melting my skin off my cold bones.

I knew I had to go out there, out into the black woods where the wild grapes trail from the trees. I just kept thinking wild grapes because "yowls" or "black night air" was too dread to let my feet walk to them. But those grapes. I could walk out into the woods for those sweet grapes. So I did.

I pushed the screen door open hard. *Bam*. Hard against the house so those night creatures knew something big and not to be messed with was coming. I wanted them to back right up and away, away from me.

"Back up and be gone, night yowlers!" I yelled.

So out I went thinking sweet wild grapes, and I came back with Stick-Person-Girl.

C. DREW LAMM

Stick-Person looked like she needed two armfuls of sweet grapes and a dozen days of sunshine. There she sat. Her eyes were night, a night with no moon. And she shivered. I whispered so as not to break her. I did everything like I was trying not to wake up a baby.

I decided to make hot chocolate like we used to have together when we were best true friends. I did it quietly though. I grabbed the kettle and picked it high off the stove before it sang. I don't think I even touched the sides of her mug when I stirred in the cocoa. I was that quiet.

She must have been froze, because when she sipped that hot chocolate she started slumping like she was melting on the inside. Her bones were losing their hold. So I held her together instead 'til her bones got solid again.

And then I waited. I kind of did and kind of didn't want to know what Stick-Person-Girl was doing howling in Sycamore Woods. Mostly I was just glad to be sitting in my kitchen again with my old best friend. Like long ago when we were just kids and had better things to think about.

I guess it made her think about stuff, too, because when she did start talking it was like rocks falling down steep land. Her words came crashing out, banging into each other, the room, and me. Words loose, rolling, and out of control. And all I could think that whole time was that she needed that purple notebook of hers. If she could only write it, it might make a heap of sense. But she just kept saying, "I don't know who I'm supposed to be anymore."

Last fall some lady from the university came to our art class to try out art therapy on us. We did these collage things where you rip anything, anything at all that catches your eye, out of magazines. Personally I thought the ripping-out part was therapy enough for me. It was about as therapeutic as anything I'd done in school. But that was just the starting part.

So anyway we had to rip out stuff that grabbed us and glue it down on blank sheets. I was so unused to being interested in a school idea I evaporated from the chair, I swear. I was just eyes and hands and I only looked at *my* collage.

Finally the teacher decided we only had a few minutes left — look at the clock and you'd know that was wrong, we still had a whole half day to put in. Anyway when I looked up, Nell Weems was staring at my collage.

"Oh, no!" said Nell Weems.

"What?" I said.

"I didn't know we were supposed to make it three-dimensional," she said back.

I'd built bridges with some of my words, and in one corner I got a group of loops twirling around each other and kind of made one of those paper

C. DREW LAMM

chains we did in kindergarten. Everyone else's collage was flat.

So Nell Weems was having a hissy fit over this three-dimensional dilemma. And I kept thinking that if she says the words *supposed to* for much longer I might smack her. I wanted to slap her hard like in the movies so she'd wake up and say, "Thanks, I needed that," and be clear-eyed, knowing who she was again, if she ever *did* know, which maybe she did when she was four years old.

And that's what I felt like in the kitchen with Stick-Person-Girl all empty and shivery and blubbering on about not knowing who she's supposed to be. I felt like slapping her to make her remember herself. To make her stop thinking of supposed-tos and start thinking about what she wanted her own life to look like.

Sometimes our inside-the-head world gets so crammed with what other people think that what we think gets squished out our ears or something. I wanted to make Stick-Person-Girl come back to her eyes and see the kettle and the plate of toast, so she could find her way back to herself. She needed to remember herself, the part of her that writes and knows things, like who her friends are and that she doesn't need boys to tell her who she is.

I thought of dragging out old magazines and making her rip out words and pictures. I wanted to *do* something. It's hard waiting for something to happen on its own.

And then Stick-Person stopped shaking and jabbering and looked up. She saw the toast on her plate. And she picked it up.

"I wish we were back in preschool again," she said. "I miss sitting in Myra's lap while she read to us. And my locker with the rabbit on it."

I just nodded. I didn't know if she was getting better or if the hot chocolate was melting her mind. She kept talking.

"It's like I knew who I was when I was four. I liked being here. I'd wake up and know who I was and be glad to be awake. Like I had a million fun things to do. And everything was nice. And we were friends."

I wanted to cry when she said the part about us.

"And my parents liked me better then," she said.

I knew what she meant. Groans didn't expect so much back then. They liked us. They got excited when we did the smallest things like dribbling blobs of paint on paper and calling them flowers or not calling them anything at all. That was okay to do. Groans were satisfied with us.

"Yeah," I said. "Don't let those old groans get to you, Stick-Person-Girl."

She smiled at me.

"And I played with boys without wondering

about stuff all the time. It didn't matter if my clothes got wrecked, and I never thought about my hair. Baby Don-Don and Checked-Wheat seemed like one of us, not so different."

"Mmmmmmmm," I said.

"We just had fun. It was all about fun and not about what other people think."

She didn't say anything more, so I said, "What happened?"

"I don't know," she said. "Tonight Nell called to say Skyler likes Rose. Mom yelled about my room and my hair was bugging me. I felt like cow pies, and I couldn't remember how I used to feel. And then I thought of you reading my notebook. I felt naked and broken. I just took off."

She stopped talking and sipped her hot chocolate for a bit. Then she looked in my eyes and said, "I saw your house through the woods — the lights on in your kitchen, and my heart broke apart. It was like looking at an old place I couldn't get back to. Like wanting to be in my little-girl self where we were friends and everything felt safe. And I couldn't get there."

"Hey, Stick-Person-Girl," I said, "you're here."

She sniffed and tears started running in little trails down her cheeks.

"I want to be here. I write to hold onto myself so I won't disappear. But it's getting harder and harder to write. And there's no time. No time for good stuff anymore."

"I'm sorry I read your journal," I said. "I shouldn't have done that."

"It's okay," she said. "If anyone was going to read my stuff, it should be you. Friends know who we are. Like you knowing I'm still just old Stick-Person-Girl. I used to hate you for that. I used to run away from your knowing me. But I need you to know me."

"Well, I miss you," I said. "And I hate seeing you disappear."

"Me too," she said.

"So what are we going to do now?" I said. "What about being seen with me at school — not cool. Should we have a secret club like in fifth grade called Secret Best Friends Club?"

Stick-Person-Girl looked really sad when I said that.

"I'm sorry, Molly-be-G," she said. "I'm really sorry. I don't know what happened. It's like you stayed where we were and I didn't. You stayed happy and I wanted more. And . . ."

"You got cool," I said.

Stick-Person sunk into her shoes. But I still had a few more things to say.

"You can't let other people rip off your good parts and make you act like some girl you don't know

C. DREW LAMM

and who looks just like everybody else. Doesn't it feel too crammed and like too small a space for you to fit?"

"It's bigger than at home," said Stick-Person. "Nothing I do is right there. Nothing feels big. At least at school I can be cool. And then it's like cool's not so cool. But I'm kind of addicted. I don't know if I can just go back on Monday and suddenly . . ."

"Go backwards!!?"

She was starting to make me hurt, and after I'd just been her bones holding her up.

"It's Skyler, right?" I said. "You care more about what you think he thinks than about friends from forever. You don't even remember I let you have that rabbit locker."

"Oh, Molly, I do care," she burst out. "Cool is butt-dumb. There. Is that better?"

"Depends," I said. "What happens when your cool friends see you talking to me, Molly-be-Gone? What then, Stick-Person-Girl?"

"Well," she said. "Maybe when they're around you could call me Ruth." Which made me laugh.

Then Ruth and I hugged and I cried, too. It had been like wandering all over the playground with night coming on, searching and searching for your old stuffed bear. It seemed like searching for so long, and like any minute a groan would come and say, "It's too late. You have to stop looking now." And then at the last minute, just as you're being dragged away, seeing an ear sticking up in the sand.

And pulling that bear out all wet, mucky, and looking like cat spit, but being so happy you don't care ice-creams what it looks like. You just hug that bear and vow to all the stars that you're never going to lose that old bear again. Never. You won't forget it or leave it behind ever again. That's how we felt.

And that was the beginning of the war. We were outnumbered of course. We were fighting the alien girls living inside our heads and racing around in our guts. But we made a pact that night to try. To stay true to ourselves and each other. It's what you have to do when you're a girl. Stick together. Remember what you love. And stay true.

The Magic Bow

The king and queen of Sagitta had raised their daughter, Princess Rowena, to be an independent young woman. From her father, she had learned oration, archery, and a dash of ruthlessness. From her mother, she had inherited a fine singing voice, a good seat on a horse, and a touch of compassion. Neither parent had ever insisted that Rowena display an interest in young men, whether real or feigned. But each was pleased and relieved when one day Rowena herself decided she would very much enjoy being married.

When she requested that they assemble all of the available barons, earls, dukes, and princes from neighboring kingdoms, the king and queen were only too happy to comply. On the appointed day, the young men arrived in great numbers. One by one they were presented to Princess Rowena. She thoroughly enjoyed the experience, admiring this one's fine head of ringlets, that one's well-muscled calf, here an exquisite set of manners, there a pair of sparkling eyes. It was not looks alone she noticed — though it must be admitted she did notice those first. Temper, too, she studied, and humor, wit, and brains. At the end, she had narrowed the prospective bridegrooms to three. These she discussed in great detail and at some length with Melisande, her lady-in-waiting and very best friend.

"Which will you choose?" Melisande asked, as eagerly as if the choice were hers.

"I don't know." Rowena shook her head. She thought for some time. Then she said, "I think perhaps I must talk to the Wood Weir."

"The Wood Weir!" gasped Melisande. "But she's a witch!"

"Of course she is," said Rowena, "and who better than a witch to help me with my future?"

It was held by those who claimed to know of such things — namely the cooks, the blacksmith, and the keeper of the royal kennels — that the Wood Weir's powers reached their peak at twilight. So that day, when the swallows retreated quietly into the barn and the bats stirred noisily in the belfry, Rowena and

Melisande rode into the forest toward the witch's home.

Rowena knew the fringes of the forest well, having ridden there many times before. But soon the familiar wide-trunked beeches gave way to alien pines and dark, drooping hemlocks. The broad leaf-littered path grew narrow and pocked with mud puddles the sun could not reach to dry. Rowena and Melisande were forced to tie up their horses and go ahead on foot.

Melisande, who had weak eyesight even in the daytime, could scarcely see in the dusky light. Being an imaginative sort, she was certain each bramble that clawed at her skirt was some bogeyman's pitchfork, each briar that snared her hair some hobgoblin's hand. As she stumbled along, she muttered an old charm against evil that her granny had taught her.

Rowena's imagination did not run to bogeymen and hobgoblins, and her vision was so sharp her father often teased that her real sire was the stableboy's cat. She strode fearlessly ahead of her friend and servant, undaunted by the briars, the mud, the thickening shadows, eagerly anticipating the Wood Weir's advice.

They smelled the Wood Weir's house before they saw it. A pungent aroma hung over the vine-covered mound squatting in a clearing and looking more like a large compost heap than anyone's home. The aroma was a strange one — sweet and acrid, sour and newly ripened, earthy and delicate — in short, it was a combination of every odor Rowena and Melisande had ever scented or imagined scenting.

"Phew." Rowena sniffed. "Old fish."

"Yum." Melisande inhaled. "Violets. At dawn. In early April."

The two young women looked at each other, shrugged, and went up to the witch's house.

There were several windows, but they were so curtained that Rowena and Melisande could not see into them. As for the door, it took them a bit of searching to find it, located as it was in the back and not the front of the house. It was a scarred and weathered door, but Rowena was amused to see that it had a rather fine knocker shaped like a frog. She knocked once, twice, three times, as she'd heard she was supposed to do, and then waited.

Several long moments passed, and then several more, until Melisande, half-hopeful, half-disappointed, said, "Perhaps she's not here. Perhaps we should come back another time."

"She's here," said Rowena. "She *must* be." From her tone Melisande could tell that her mistress was more anxious than she'd suspected.

Still more time passed, and then, at last, they heard an irritable creaking as the door opened. A yellow light streamed out, emanating from several

MARILYN SINGER

glowing lanterns. Standing in its path was a trim woman of medium height in a deep green gown. Her hair, generously streaked with gray, hung loosely around her shoulders. Her face was the kind to which few would give a second glance. Her eyes were the kind from which few could tear their glance away.

"So," she said, blocking the entrance. "So. What brings the Princess Rowena and her lady-in-waiting to my door at this hour?" She stared piercingly at the two young women before her.

Melisande flinched under her gaze and took one step back. Rowena smiled and took two steps forward. "I believe you already know," she said. "But if you do not, let us in and I shall tell you."

At such boldness the Wood Weir let out a short loud laugh. "I believe I should like to hear your version," she said, and ushered them inside.

The room they entered was neat and spare. There were no talismans on the walls, no charms on the floor, no sign of a raven or a black cat. There isn't even a broomstick, noted Melisande, though no doubt there must be one around someplace if only to keep the house so clean. In short, the Wood Weir's home was so surprisingly ordinary Melisande did not know whether to be more at ease or less so. What kind of witch was this to display no symbols of her craft? Pondering this question, Melisande perched on a low stool in the corner from which she could both observe the proceedings and avoid the Wood Weir's scrutiny.

Rowena, on the other hand, oblivious to both the decor and the lack of magical paraphernalia in the Wood Weir's parlor, sat down in a more comfortable chair directly across from the older woman. Immediately she began to tell the witch why she had come. She used all her eloquence to describe the three promising suitors: first, the silver-tongued baron whose gifts were so exactly to Rowena's tastes, whose compliments matched so precisely what Rowena wished to hear that she wondered if he also knew of the magical arts; second, the handsome duke, who bore an astounding resemblance to the small statue of Adonis Rowena kept in her bedchamber, well hidden from her parents' eyes; last, the charming Prince Cyprian, not so gracious or handsome as the other two, but possessing a certain "something"— though just what Rowena could not say. She paused then and laughed, remembering what Melisande's response had been when they'd discussed the prince. "Well, he does have an awfully nice smile," her friend had said.

The Wood Weir did not laugh with her. In fact, she made no sound at all. Her silence stopped Rowena's laughter. The princess took a deep breath, stifled a hiccup, and shifted forward in her seat. Then, with urgency, she asked, "Can you tell me which one is the husband for me?"

"No," the Wood Weir replied.

"No?" Rowena was startled.

"No. I cannot tell you. You must learn it yourself."

"How? How must I learn it? Can you tell me that?"

This time the Wood Weir nodded slowly. "You must disguise your name and station, but not your sex, and travel to each suitor's court. There you will challenge your baron, your duke, and your prince to an archery contest. You will learn all you need to know when you win."

"When I win? I am a good archer, but that does not mean I will always win."

The Wood Weir moved with surprising swiftness toward the corner where Melisande sat. The younger woman shrank away, but the Wood Weir ignored her. She reached behind Melisande and pulled out a longbow, dark and plain save for a single strange crest burned into the upper limb. Holding out the bow, she faced Rowena. "You shall always win with this," she said.

Rowena hesitated a moment before crossing to the witch and taking the bow from her hand. She studied its height and balance, then pulled the string to test its draw weight. It's a good bow, she thought, well made and sturdy. But it does not appear extraordinary. "What arrows shall I use?" she asked, wondering if perhaps the Wood Weir had not yet given her all of the equipment or information she needed.

"Any you like. They shall all fly true."

Feeling somewhat skeptical, Rowena nonetheless thanked the Wood Weir heartily and asked, "What can I give you in return?"

"Money will do nicely," the Wood Weir said with a small smile.

Rowena took a handful of coins from her pocket and gave them to the woman. "Come, Melisande," she said, turning to her friend. "We'd better prepare at once for our journey."

Now Melisande was not feeling skeptical at all. She had peered into the space behind her before she'd sat down and she knew beyond a doubt that it had been empty — there had been no bow nor anything else hidden there at all. Swallowing hard, Melisande rose and edged toward her mistress, keeping as far away from the Wood Weir as she could.

But just when she thought she was safely out of the witch's way, the woman reached out and grasped her arm. "Here is something for you, too, little servant girl." The woman held out her palm. On it lay a small leather case.

Melisande did not want to touch the gift. But she could not stop her hands from seizing the case and shoving it into her pocket.

"Use it well," the Wood Weir called after her as she bolted out the door.

Later, when Rowena asked, she would say she'd lost the gift, whatever it was, on their lantern-lit ride back to the palace. In fact, she had tried several times to toss it away, but she could not do it. I'll leave it in the pocket of this gown and leave the gown behind, and I won't think of it all the journey long, which will make it as good as lost, she decided.

What gowns Melisande and Rowena would wear on their journey required some careful planning. In the end, Rowena had her seamstress sew some simple garments patterned after those worn by a pair of itinerant cartographers visiting the court — sisters who were delighted to be of further service by providing maps so that Rowena and Melisande would not get lost on their way. Besides the clothing, Rowena purchased wigs and powder, rouge and even false eyebrows from a company of actors her parents patronized.

As for her parents, Rowena told them of the proposed journey and its reason, but she did not tell of her visit to the Wood Weir nor of the magic bow. "I want to see what the guests are like as hosts," she said, paraphrasing an old proverb.

Her mother was not pleased with the idea. "You may not like what you see," she warned her daughter.

"I believe that is the point, my dear," the king told his wife with a fond smile. He kissed Rowena and bade her a safe journey. The queen did the same, slipping into Rowena's hands a purse of gold should she find herself in need of it.

Then, donning their new dresses, wigs, and other means of disguise, and securing the magic bow in the case attached to Rowena's horse's saddle, the princess and her servant rode out from the castle toward their first destination.

The baron's estate was as fair and large as he had described. To gain entrance to the manor, Rowena had invented a brief but intriguing tale, which she told first to the gatekeeper and then to the hierarchy of footmen, chamberlains, and the like. With her usual skill at storytelling, she said that she and her companion were visitors from a country across the sea. She had heard much of the skill with bow and arrow possessed by the lords and ladies of these lands and had come to try her luck against them.

"The lords and *ladies*?" said the baron when word reached him of his new guest. "I know of no ladies whose skill at archery approaches that of any man. I'll not see her."

But when his secretary mentioned the fat purse of gold this bold, young woman was willing to wager, he reconsidered. "Perhaps I should meet this foreigner after all," he said. "Let her come to dinner tonight."

The task of extending his invitation, and also of entertaining the foreigners prior to the meal, fell to the baron's two sisters. These young women, both so reserved they made Melisande feel outspoken, led the guests around the estate, pointing out the many beautiful objects their brother had collected: tapestries, paintings, marble statues, porcelain plates, ivory chess sets, cloisonné urns, and other knickknacks. Rowena exclaimed over each treasure and commented that the baron had sublime taste. The sisters agreed that his taste was indeed wonderful, but they showed no pride in their brother when they said it. Nor did they show much enthusiasm in recounting the stories behind each acquisition. They related the tales in flat, uninflected voices as if they had been forced to tell them too many times before. Rowena, by contrast, in response to the sisters' gentle prodding, spun inventive fables about her adventures in so lively a fashion the two young women were left wide-eyed and flushed with excitement.

Near the end of the tour, they came to the library, a spacious room paneled in rare wood and lined floor to ceiling with even rarer books. Rowena, who liked to read, was truly astounded. She plucked several volumes from the shelves and leafed through them with delight, while Melisande squinted nearsightedly over her shoulder, trying to make out the words.

"How lucky you are to have all these books to read!" Rowena exclaimed to the sisters. "Which are your favorites?"

"Oh, we haven't read any of them," the older sister said quietly.

"Our brother feels it is a waste of our time and will give us a terrible squint," said the younger, glancing with embarrassment at Melisande when she realized what she'd just said.

Rowena's brow furrowed in surprise and dismay, but she made no reply.

"Tell us more about your travels," the older put in quickly. "Yes, do," added the younger, and Rowena obliged.

The rest of the day passed swiftly, and soon it was time for dinner. The two sisters led Rowena and Melisande to the dining hall, where a long table was set with a service of gold. The other guests were already in their places. Rowena was seated at the baron's right-hand side, Melisande much farther down the table. Even here I am seen as a servant, Melisande thought, wondering why that position had never bothered her before. The younger sister sat next to Rowena, the elder across from her. They chatted pleasantly until their host arrived.

Dressed in a suit of rich burgundy velvet, he greeted his guests, scattering compliments like petals. Several lords and ladies thanked him for gifts he'd recently bestowed on them. His skill with words and his obvious generosity endeared him to Rowena once more. When he finished this exchange of pleasantries, he clapped his hands and announced, "I understand we have a new guest tonight." He turned to Rowena with a smile. "You have traveled quite a distance to reach our fair land, have you not?"

"And well worth the trip it was to be among your company," came Rowena's formal reply.

"Would you care to travel such a distance?" the baron asked his youngest sister.

Still excited by Rowena's tales, she replied incautiously, "Yes, I would."

"Why, my little mouse, you could scarcely find your front gate without losing your way," he told her, and his guests tittered. He waved his hand to stop their laughter. "And why *should* she need to know the way? What could she find outside more beautiful than the treasures in her home? For it is man's duty to provide beauty for his women's pleasure and it is woman's duty to be ever beautiful for her men," he declaimed.

The guests applauded. The younger sister bit her lip and lowered her eyes. Along the table Rowena and Melisande exchanged troubled glances.

"Is it true that you are an archer?" the baron asked, turning back to Rowena.

"Yes," she said coolly. "I wish to challenge you to a contest. I have gold to wager." She took out her purse and plunked it on the table.

"You would do better challenging my sister." He nodded at the elder of the two. "The first and last time she drew a bow we had to call the surgeon to mend her hand."

The laughter rose again. The sister reddened and frowned.

The baron grew more serious. "It is not the custom in our domain for a man and a woman to compete in sport. But since you are from across the sea, and as you seem so eager"— he eyed the fat purse — "I will accept your challenge." He motioned, and a servant came forward to place an equally large purse next to Rowena's. "Dine well, my friends. We shall have gold for dessert," the baron announced, and he beckoned his servants to begin serving the meal.

Because it was summer, there was still ample daylight after dinner by which to hold the contest outdoors. So all of the guests moved to the archery range, where freshly painted targets stood on a neatly trimmed green with flags set at varying distances. The targets' colored circles — white, black, blue, red, and, at the center, gold — shone brightly in the sun. The servant bore the purses on a gleaming silver tray,

MARILYN SINGER

while the guests eagerly made private wagers among themselves as to the number of points by which Rowena would lose.

The baron allowed Rowena to choose the target and to take some practice shots. To her growing alarm, not one of her arrows hit nearer the center than the black circle. The bets against her escalated.

"Oh, Melisande, what have I gotten us into?" she whispered to her friend standing nearby.

"Don't worry. The bow will work. I am sure of it," Melisande said.

Rowena nodded firmly, but inside she was far less certain.

Then the baron declared that the contest would officially begin. A coin toss declared him the first archer. He and Rowena would alternate, each shooting three arrows at a time, and each advancing nearer to the target every two rounds, until they had shot eighteen arrows in all. Whoever received the highest score would be declared the winner.

The baron stepped to the first flag and raised his bow confidently. He shot well — his first two arrows pierced the blue circle, his third the red. By contrast, Rowena could do no better than the blue ring — and that only once.

In the second round, she scored higher than the baron, and in the third, she equaled him. But still she was behind.

"If you would perhaps care to concede now, you may take back your purse and go on your way with no rancor on my part," the baron offered, trying — and failing — to conceal his smirk.

"I do not care to concede," Rowena said tightly.

"Very well," said the baron. He drew his bow, and, in quick succession, made two golds. The audience laughed and applauded and sighed only a little when his third shot struck the red.

Rowena clenched her teeth. Concentrate, she told herself, and released an arrow. A red. Good. Again. A gold. Once more. Another gold. The crowd began to murmur. Let them, she thought. She felt stronger now, more at ease. Yet she still had no great faith in the bow and she was still losing.

When her turn came again, she felt a weariness steal upon her. No, she said to herself. I can win this contest. I *will* win it.

The change happened so quietly, she scarcely took note of it. The bow she held was no longer an object distant from her. It had become an extension of her arms, her trunk, her legs, of the very earth itself. A force flowed from the ground up through her body out to her fingers and into the bowstring. She knew that each and every arrow she let fly would go nowhere but the target's dead center.

The crowd's buzz grew louder. The baron's eyes

narrowed. His brow furrowed. No longer smiling, he stepped to the flag and drew his bow. One by one his final three arrows hit the center, leaving no room at all for Rowena's. The audience, sensing victory for their host, chattered noisily.

Rowena did not hear them. As if in a dream, she drew her bow and shot — and every one of her arrows split each of the baron's neatly down its shaft.

The crowd gasped and fell silent. It was a long moment before the baron, a vein pulsing furiously in his neck, hissed, "Impossible. No woman can shoot like that — nor any man either — unless she cheats. We do not deal kindly with cheaters here, be they countrymen or foreigners from across the sea." He paused, glaring. Then, without turning his head, he bellowed, "Seize that bow! And take this woman and her companion to the dungeon until we decide what is to be done with them!"

The next thing Rowena knew, guards tore the magic bow from her hands and roughly dragged her and Melisande away.

Soon they sat, arms around one another, on grimy straw mats in a dark, dank cell.

"This is my fault," Rowena apologized. "I have gotten us into this. Now I must get us out."

"This is the Wood Weir's fault. It is her magic that got us here," Melisande corrected, trying to sound brave and loyal. But as she spoke, a scent like violets wafted into the room, and she found herself curiously unable to believe her own words.

"Well, in any event, the Wood Weir's prediction was true. She said I'd learn what I needed to know when I won the contest. I have learned that under no circumstances do I wish to marry that baron."

"The swine!" Melisande agreed hotly.

"Odd though, how one can be so easily fooled by a few fine words and pretty trinkets," Rowena said pensively.

Melisande could think of no comforting phrases to offer in reply, so she just patted the princess's shoulder and said nothing at all.

Hours passed. How many more would have gone by before the baron would have freed Rowena and Melisande or sent them to a worse fate they were fortunate never to learn. While the lord of the manor slept soundly in his canopied bed, his youngest sister came and opened their cell door. Warning them to follow swiftly and silently, she led them up and out of the dungeon to the stables where their horses, saddled and bridled, waited. Waiting there, too, was the older sister. She handed Rowena her magic bow and the two purses of gold. "Go quickly before our brother discovers you have gone," she said.

Rowena thanked them, then, concerned, asked if they would be in any danger.

"Do not worry. He will not put us in such a

prison as you have been," the older sister said rather wryly.

The younger sister agreed, but wistfully added, "We wish we could leave, too."

"Perhaps one day you will," Rowena replied.

She and Melisande led their horses from the stables. The sisters opened the gates. Then the princess and her lady-in-waiting rode away, guided only by starlight.

The journey to the duke's palace was a long one, and both Rowena and Melisande were grateful for the maps they carried and the extra purse of gold. They found that the latter not only paid for food and lodging, but that it quickly silenced the innkeepers who looked askance at women traveling alone, changing their mockery into fawning respect.

Gold, too, eased their way into the duke's presence once Rowena realized they might avoid the hierarchy of servants if she paid the porter to summon the one who could take them directly to his lord.

It was this servant now who led Rowena and Melisande through the halls to the duke's sitting room. When the servant opened the carved doors, Rowena felt her breath catch in her throat. Bordered by the doorway like a painting in a frame, the duke, dressed in white and silver, was lying languidly on a rose-colored chaise, and he was even more handsome

THE MAGIC BOW

than Rowena had recalled. It was not until she entered the room that she noticed he was not alone. A woman, older and not as beautiful, but bearing a striking resemblance to the duke, sat in a nearby chair, reading to him from a book of poetry.

"Don't stop, Mother," he said when she broke off in the middle of a sentence.

"We have visitors, my son."

"They will not mind waiting until you finish the poem," said the duke, giving Rowena and Melisande a dazzling smile. "Will they?"

"No. Please go on," Rowena said.

The duchess nodded and continued. It was a rather long poem and a tiresome one, Rowena thought. She had ample time to glance about the room. It was not filled with many precious knickknacks, as all of the baron's rooms had been. There were no statues or urns or tapestries. But there were several paintings on the walls — and every one of them was a portrait of the duke, his mother, or the two of them together.

Rowena surreptitiously nudged Melisande so she, too, would notice this odd collection. But Melisande was listening rather intently to the poem, which was about a boy who saved his mother from a witch's wrath. It was just the sort of melodramatic ode she used to like. But this one sounded absurdly false. Not all witches are like that. Not all witches are evil, she thought, as a violet perfume drifted through the room and just as quickly disappeared.

"Well read, Mother," the duke said when she'd at last finished. "Was it not?" He turned to Rowena and Melisande. They nodded politely. "Now, what brings you fair ladies to our duchy?" He cocked his head charmingly to listen.

So Rowena began to tell him, but she had not gotten very far when he interrupted to ask his mother if the hairdresser was coming today.

"No, my dear, tomorrow," his mother told him. "Ah." He turned back to Rowena. "Pardon me, do go on."

Uncertain as to whether he'd heard any of her tale. Rowena began anew — and was again interrupted. "Do you think I should ask for the same style, or the new one the Earl of Abingdon has popularized?" asked the duke.

"Oh, do try the new style. It will show off your cheekbones to even better advantage," his mother replied.

"I believe you're right." He looked at Rowena. "Please continue."

Gathering her patience, she did and managed, after only three more interruptions, to complete her story.

"Archery? Could we not fence instead? I'm quite partial to fencing," said the duke.

"I cannot fence."

"Pity." He frowned, and the expression did little for his cheekbones.

"Dear, I believe you should accept this young woman's wager. After all, you are nearly as good with a bow and arrow as you are with a foil," his mother put in.

"I am at that, aren't I?" he said thoughtfully. "Very well. I will accept your challenge — after my hairdresser's appointment tomorrow. One should always look one's best for a crowd," he added without a dash of irony.

"Of course," agreed Rowena with more than a cupful.

After a perfectly pleasant and uneventful evening and an equally pleasant and uneventful morning, Rowena and Melisande went out to the duke's archery range. Only two people were waiting there, and Rowena began to wonder if she had misheard the appointed hour. A servant assured her that she had not.

"Well, where is everyone then?"

"They will be here. They are aware of the duke's habits."

"Meaning?"

"The duke goes by Jupiterian time, mistress."

The euphemism was vaguely familiar. "In other words, he's always late?" asked Rowena.

"Just that," said the servant with a slight smile.

One hour later, the spectators began to arrive. An hour past that, the duke appeared with his retinue. He wore an elaborate coat sewn with pearls and on his head was an absurdly plumed hat to which his hand strayed self-consciously several times.

Melisande looked at it and tried not to laugh. Rowena tried not to sigh. She had begun to doubt her judgment in the baron's palace and now she doubted it all the more.

The contest, if such it could be called, was anticlimactic. Rowena did not shoot as well as she had against the baron. She did not have to. The duke was a rather mediocre bowman.

"I knew I should have canceled this contest. After what that butcher did to my hair, I'm so annoyed I can't concentrate at all," he muttered to his mother, but loud enough for Rowena to hear. "Besides, I'm coming down with a head cold. And I told you I was better at fencing anyway." The way his lower lip pouted and his chin jutted out erased any resemblance to Adonis Rowena had once noted.

"Come inside, dear. Peter will bring you some sugared barley water, and I'll give you a foot massage," the duchess promised.

"Would you, Mother? You're much better at it than he is. You shall have to teach it to the Princess Rowena when we marry. I'm sure she'd be happy to learn it, though of course she'll never have your touch."

"I daresay that's probably true," said the duchess with a little laugh.

They walked away without a word or a backward glance at Rowena. Melisande, who had been trying hard not to laugh, giggled so hard she had to stuff her sleeve into her mouth.

"This is not amusing," said Rowena rather mournfully. "I could have married that fop or that tyrant before him."

"But you didn't," Melisande reminded her. "And you won't."

"True." Rowena took a deep breath and juggled the two purses of gold in her hands. "Shall we see if there is more to Prince Cyprian than his nice smile?"

"Let's," said Melisande.

And without bidding their host good-bye, they were on their way.

It took well over a fortnight and several adventures, not all of them enjoyable, before Rowena and Melisande wearily arrived in Prince Cyprian's kingdom, a modest realm largely given over to the cultivation of apple orchards. Rowena did not need to tip the porter or the other servants. She and Melisande did not even need to go to the castle gates. They found the prince outside them, in his shirtsleeves, high up in an apple tree, helping the chief gardener pluck unripe fruit.

Rowena stood silently, admiring his quiet concentration and the deftness of his strong hands. Only when he finished did he look her way and call down, "Now the remaining apples will be bigger and sweeter, and the tree will grow better."

"Why? Why will it grow better?" Rowena asked, entering the conversation as easily as he'd begun it.

"It will not have to put all its strength into bearing so much fruit, and its branches will not become damaged from drooping."

"Really? That's interesting."

"Do you think so?"

"Yes. I think I should like to know even more about apple trees," said Rowena.

"I should be pleased to tell you." The prince smiled then, and Rowena could not fail to notice that it was a very nice smile indeed. Leaping down from the tree, he dusted off his hands, donned his coat, and offered his arms to her and to Melisande.

Melisande demurred, saying she'd prefer to rest under a shady tree. But Rowena took his arm, and he led her away to stroll through the orchard. As they walked, he spoke of his plans to improve it, and he asked Rowena's advice on many of his ideas as though she were an old and valued friend.

"But how rude of me. I have not let you talk

about yourself and what has brought you to my home," he said when they came back to where Melisande sat waiting.

Rowena, who did not find him rude at all, began to tell her time-worn tale. But when it came time to challenge him to the contest, she hesitated.

Melisande tried to prompt her. "Do you care for archery, my lord?" she asked.

"I do indeed. It is my favorite sport," he answered. "Are you an archer, too?"

"Not I. But my friend is." She nodded at Rowena. "And quite a fine one. She has triumphed over barons and dukes."

The prince turned to Rowena with another smile. "Excellent! Perhaps you would oblige me in a match sometime during your stay."

"Perhaps," Rowena replied.

In the days that followed, she rambled often with the prince in the orchard and rode by his side in the fields. He taught her how to prune a tree. She taught him the lyrics to several lively songs. But not once did she pick up her bow — and she knew perfectly well why. She was in no hurry to find out what he would be like when he lost the match. She was certain, given her recent experiences, that no matter how pleasant he seemed to be before the contest — and there was no doubt that he seemed very, very pleasant — he would prove a disappointment after.

"Perhaps things will not turn out as badly as you expect," Melisande suggested when Rowena told her this.

"True. They may turn out worse," said Rowena.

But one morning, when the prince himself brought up the topic again, Rowena decided she could put him off no longer, and she agreed to a match that very afternoon.

At three o'clock, she walked sadly to the archery range — which was nothing more than a faded target tacked to the stump of a tree. More mournfully still, before a small but enthusiastic audience, she let fly shot upon perfect shot. When she won, she lowered her bow and, holding her arms stiffly at her side, steeled herself against the prince's reaction.

She was stunned to discover that he was smiling. "Your companion did not do you justice. You are not a fine archer. You are a brilliant one. I'm honored that you deigned to match your bow against the likes of mine." He bowed to her, and the crowd applauded vigorously.

Melisande nearly clapped her hands as well with relief and glee.

But Rowena could only nod her head curtly and say, "Thank you."

Prince Cyprian's mouth kept smiling, but his blue eyes looked quizzical. And when Rowena said she was fatigued and asked his leave to retire, his eyes turned gray with unspoken sadness.

She lay on her bed for the rest of the day and well past dinnertime.

"What on earth is the matter?" Melisande asked over and over. "You should be rejoicing. You have found your husband at last."

Rowena would not answer. She did not know what was troubling her. But she was certain that she could not face Prince Cyprian again until she did.

When Melisande — and the rest of the court — had fallen asleep, she slipped from the room to stroll in the orchard. There, as luck would have it, she found the prince.

"Is the moon keeping you from your dreams as it is keeping me from mine?" He glanced up at the full silver sphere in the sky. "It is so bright."

"No. It's not the moon," Rowena answered gravely. And all at once she understood what was wrong and how to make it right. "Will you grant me a rematch, my lord?" she asked.

"With pleasure," he replied, without questioning her request.

"When will it suit your convenience?"

"I can think of no better time than now. Shall I summon a servant to fetch your bow?"

"I'd rather use one from your collection, if you will allow it."

"I will — and most gladly," he replied, his eyes shining warmly in the moonlight.

They set a longer contest than before — thirty-six arrows each. Never before had Rowena found herself so evenly matched. First it was she who was winning. Then it was the prince. Though she no longer had the Wood Weir's magic to help her, it seemed she had a new kind born of her own talent and will. Her fingers tingled. Her arms ached. Sweat poured from her brow. But she laughed aloud with the thrill of a game well played, a battle fairly fought. And when the last arrow had been shot and the points tallied, she found that she had really and truly won — more than she'd ever hoped to win before.

Grinning, Cyprian caught her hands to whirl her merrily around.

"Wait." She stopped him. "There is something I must tell you."

He pressed his fingers to her lips. "There is no need," he said. "I, too, have visited the Wood Weir, Princess Rowena, to ask how I may win your love."

Rowena gasped. "You knew! All along you knew that it was I and that my bow was magic!"

Cyprian blushed, though in the moonlight Rowena could not see. "Yes. I confess I did."

"And what else did she tell you? What did she say you must do to win my love?"

"She told me to contend with you willingly as an equal and to accept defeat gracefully, but never condescend to let you win. This I did gladly, though it troubled me that you would not trust in your own talent and my goodwill."

"It is hard to trust in a man's goodwill when so few men offer it," Rowena said.

"May I ever be one of those few men," Cyprian avowed with a smile, which Rowena returned.

Then she took him in her arms, and they were embracing still when Melisande, who had awakened to find her mistress gone, came upon them there under a tree. Though she could not see them clearly, she knew well enough what they were about and she tiptoed away before they knew she'd been there.

Back in the bedchamber, Melisande stroked the strange crest on the magic bow Rowena had left behind. My mistress's quest has ended, she said to herself, and therefore so has mine. But she wondered why the thought made her sad as well as joyous.

Then suddenly she smelled an odor that could only have been violets and she heard the Wood Weir's voice saying, "Here is something for you, too, little servant girl. Use it well." She found herself reaching into the pocket of her gown and drawing out a small leather case. "But I was sure I left it at home," she said with wonder. Fingers trembling, she opened the case.

Inside lay a pair of plain, gold-rimmed spectacles. Melisande picked them up with a breathless little laugh. She suspected that once she put them on more than the room would become clear. And of course, she was right.

After Rowena and Cyprian's wedding — a simple but lively affair at which the wedding cake was a huge apple pie — Melisande, the maid of honor, bid her mistress a fond good-bye. Then she went off with the Wood Weir to become her valued apprentice. It is said in the years to come she surpassed the skill of her esteemed teacher — especially in the field of match-making.

It is said, too, that Rowena and her prince lived long and fruitful lives, and though all of their children had many different talents, every one of them was excellent with an arrow and a bow.

About the Authors

JENNIFER ARMSTRONG is the author of over thirty books for children and young adults. Among her award-winning titles are *Steal Away, Chin Yu Min and the Ginger Cat, Hugh Can Do, The Dreams of Mairhe Mehan,* and *Black-Eyed Susan.* She grew up outside of New York City and was a teenager at the time of the Bicentennial, although she never dressed up as the Statue of Liberty. She lives now in Saratoga Springs, New York, with her husband, author James Howard Kunstler, two dogs, and a cat. She has indeed been to Paris.

MARIAN FLANDRICK BRAY has written sixteen novels for kids, including a series about the famous collie Lassie. She grew up on the border of East Los Angeles. She has worked as a horse wrangler, barnyard zookeeper, and newspaper reporter. Currently she is a library assistant and on call 24-hours a day with the Orange County Search and Rescue Team. She lives in Santa Ana, California, with her husband, daughter, two dogs, a cat, two chinchillas, a colony of guinea pigs, and a black Morgan mare.

PENI R. GRIFFIN is the author of nine books for children, including *Switching Well* and the Edgar-nominated mystery *The Treasure Bird*. A self-proclaimed Air Force brat, she says her childhood was spent reading and taking long car trips as her family moved — from Texas to Alaska to Iowa to Maryland and, finally, back to Texas. She lives today in a 90-year-old house in San Antonio, Texas, with her husband, Michael D. Griffin; a housemate, Michael Christy; and three cats.

M. E. KERR was born in Auburn, New York. She attended the University of Missouri. Currently living in East Hampton, New York, she is the author of numerous young adult and adult novels, including *Deliver us from Evie* and *Me Me Me Me Me: Not a Novel*. She has been called "one of the pioneers in realistic fiction for teenagers" in an award she received from the ALA's Young Adult Library Services Association.

C. DREW LAMM grew up in Guelph Ontario, Canada, where she lived down the street from children's book author, Robert Munsch, and across the river from author Jean Little. Ms. Lamm is herself the author of several picture books for children, including *Anni-ranni and Mollymishi, the Wild-Haired Doll* and *Cottontail at Clover Crescent;* and two upcoming books, *Pirates* and *The Prog Frince.* She lives with her husband, Steve, and her daughter, Ellery Rose, in Connecticut. She says "'Stay True' is a mixture of girls/women I've known, been, imagined, and hoped to be."

ANNE MAZER grew up in a family of writers in upstate New York. She has studied art and French literature; traveled in Europe and Asia; and worked at a variety of jobs. Her children's books range from picture books (*The Salamander Room*) to middle grade novels (*The Accidental Witch*) to young adult short-story collections (*A Sliver of Glass*). She has edited three well-known anthologies, including *America Street.* Her story, "The Transformations of Cindy R.," is not based on her own experience. She has never had a fairy godmother or danced with Prince Charming at a ball. She lives in Ithaca, New York, with her two children, two computers, and several imaginary pets.

NORMA FOX MAZER has written twenty-five novels for children and young adults, including three with her husband, Harry Mazer. Her novel *A Figure of Speech* was a National Book Award nominee; *After the Rain* was a Newbery Honor book, a *Horn Book* Fanfare book, an ALA Notable Children's Book, and an ALA Best Books for Young Adults (as were many of her other books). Several of her books have been on ALA 100 Best of the Best lists. Ms. Mazer's most recent book is *When She Was Good* (Scholastic Press/Arthur A. Levine Books). She divides her time between a home in central New York State and New York City.

ANDREA DAVIS PINKNEY is the author of ten books for children, including several books illustrated by Caldecott-Honor-winner Brian Pinkney, Ms. Pinkney's husband. They are: *Bill Pickett: Rodeo Ridin' Cowboy*, an ALA Notable Children's Book; *Dear Benjamin Banneker*, a NCSS-CBS Notable Book; *Alvin Ailey*, winner of the Parents' Choice Gold Medal; and *Seven Candles for Kwanzaa*, an American Bookseller Pick of the Lists. Ms. Pinkney's novel, *Hold Fast to Dreams*, was also named an American Bookseller Pick of the Lists. Her most recent work is *Solo Girl*, a chapter book.

MARILYN SINGER was born in the Bronx and now lives in Brooklyn, New York, with her husband, Steve Aronson. As a writer, she appreciates being called "versatile." She is the author of over fifty books for children and young adults, whose works include poetry, fantasies, mysteries, realistic fiction, nonfiction, and picture books. *Stay True* is the first short-story collection she has compiled and edited. In addition to her writing, Ms. Singer enjoys bird-watching, hiking, going to the movies and theatre, playing CD-ROM adventure games, and training her standard poodle, Easy, for obedience shows. Currently, she hosts the America Online Children's Writers Chat.

MARION DE BOOY WENTZIEN has published over 300 short stories in a variety of national publications, including *Story, Seventeen,* and *The San Francisco Chronicle*. In 1991 she won the University of Missouri-Kansas City New Letters Award, and she was a PEN Syndicated Fiction competition winner in 1986 and 1987. Her short story "Phoenix" was chosen to be read on National Public Radio's program *The Sound of Writing*. She lives in Saratoga, California.

RITA WILLIAMS-GARCIA was born in Queens, New York, where she lives today with her daughters, Michelle, age 13, and Stephanie, age 9. Her novels for young adults, noted for their realistic depiction of contemporary African-American teens, include *Like Sisters on the Homefront,* a Coretta Scott King Honor Book, an

ALA Best Book, a *Horn Book* Best Book, and a *Booklist* Best Book; *Blue Tights* and *Fast Talk on a Slow Track*, both of which have won Parents' Choice Awards. All three of her books have been selected for NYPL Books for the Teen Age and YALSA Quick Picks for Reluctant Readers. In 1997 Ms. Williams-Garcia was awarded the PEN Norma Klein Award for her body of work. In addition to writing children's books she works as a full-time manager at a marketing services company.